M000040440

MISTER HOLLYWOOD

A PLAYER ROMANCE

MIKA LANE

HEADLANDS PUBLISHING

Join Mika's Insider Group
www.mikalane.com
Contact Mika

Copyright© 2018 by Mika Lane
Headlands Publishing
4200 Park Blvd. #244
Oakland, CA 94602

Mister Hollywood is a work of fiction. Names, characters, (most) places, and incidents are either the product of the author's creativity or are used fictitiously. Any resemblance to actual persons, living or dead, events, or locales is entirely coincidental.
All rights reserved. This book or any portion thereof may not be reproduced or used in any manner whatsoever without the express written permission of the publisher except for the use of quotations in a book review.

ISBN ebook 978-1-948369-18-3
ISBN print 978-1-948369-19-0

CHAPTER 1

BELLE

The pink fabric strained—I honestly didn't know how it didn't completely rupture—across what looked like two giant balloons. But they weren't balloons. They were two of the biggest freaking boobs I'd ever seen.

I didn't normally spend much time looking at other women's boobs. After all, I had my own. And while they were nothing to write home about, when I checked them out in the mirror at home they were nice enough, if on the small side. No complaints on my part.

"They're...nice, Jackie," I said to my best friend at work. Actually, she was my best friend, period.

She looked down on her protuberant chest, nodding in happy appreciation of my compliment. As if she, or anyone else, could miss the enhancements.

Could she actually see her feet over those massive new mounds of silicone?

"Aren't they great? I am soooo freaking thrilled with my new girls." She cupped them and they poured over the tops of her hands.

I looked around the car dealership, where I was the receptionist and all-round office gopher bitch. From the other side of the showroom, where he sat over-looking our every move, our boss, Ted, caught Jackie feeling herself up. He frowned for a moment, shook his head, and went back to the paperwork on his desk.

The poor man tried to keep all of us in line, but his efforts were usually futile. Car salesmen and women are typically a bit on the crazy side, although that didn't begin to explain Jackie's eccentricities. But when you're top salesperson by a factor of five, you could pretty much do whatever the hell you wanted to at work.

And Jackie clearly wanted to keep talking about her new boobs. I could deal with that—after all, she was that good of a friend.

"Hold on a sec, would you?" I asked, as I picked up a call and directed it to our service department.

I returned my attention to Jackie and her new boobs. "So. How are you feeling? All the stitches gone?"

She leaned closer to me, as if she were all of sudden going for privacy. "Not yet. The doctor said he wants to make sure there's as little scarring as possible. I need to keep them bound up for a bit longer. So, no test-driving yet, but I can't wait to try them out on some lucky guy. It'll be so freaking hot."

Breaking off our conversation, she scanned the showroom like a shark looking for her next meal. "Gotta go!" she said, thrusting her chest out and making for a couple bickering over a red convertible.

Jackie was like a shrink for people looking for cars. The car-whisperer, I called her. Somehow, she got the most belligerent folks to calm down, listen to her, trust her, and then of course, buy from her. That's how she came to be so loaded.

Not that I begrudged the woman anything. Lord, no. She worked her ass off, and she was generous, to boot. I mean, she had twins at home whose dad did not pay a cent in child support. Obviously, she had to make things happen. And, god bless her, more often than not she paid for me, too, like when we had a girls' nights out.

So I got back to the phones and my other glamorous responsibilities like checking on the clogged toilet in the women's room. I also directed a new customer to Starla, Jackie's archrival in both the boob and sales category. At one time, Starla had been the lead salesperson, powered by a breathy voice, big blue eyes, and an ass that was almost certainly surgically enhanced. But when Jackie came to town, she stole the honor right from under her so fast that everyone's heads at the dealership had spun. And Starla had pretty much hated Jackie ever since. The rivalry was epic.

At noon on the dot, Jackie headed my way for lunch.

"Usual place?" I asked after I hung up, grabbing my purse.

"Of course. Let's go." Jackie said, leading me to her custom-painted gold-tone Mercedes.

That's how she rolled.

The smell of a House of Waffles sort of restaurant had always done something to me. Maybe it was going there as a kid, or maybe it was the comfort of late-night drunken meals in college, when I'd earned my useless art degree. Whatever it was, we'd no sooner walked in and I was instantly in my happy place. How was it that a smell from the past could be so damn good?

And even though House of Waffles specialized in breakfast foods, they had so much more, including an amazing Monte Cristo sandwich I ordered every single time I went there. That day was no exception.

"Hey, ladies. Good to see you. The usual?" our regular waitress asked.

Jackie looked at me and rolled her eyes. "You're getting the same damn thing as always, aren't you?"

The waitress laughed, scribbling on her order pad. "Don't give the girl a hard time. She knows what she likes. What'll you have, Jackie?"

"Ummm…" Jackie said, flipping through the menu, as if she didn't know by heart everything they served there. As much as she gave me a hard time for ordering the same thing all the time, she did the same thing, herself.

"I'll have the Greek salad," she finally said as she handed her menu back to the waitress. As if there really were a decision to be made.

The waitress clicked her pen and nodded." All righty, ladies. Be right back with your ice teas."

"So how are ya?" Jackie asked from across the booth, where her newly acquired breasts nearly rested on the tabletop.

I shrugged. "Good, I guess. Why?"

"Eh. I don't know," Jackie said with an inquisitive look. "I thought you looked a bit frazzled this morning. Did your classes already start up?"

Did I look that bad?

"No. I haven't enrolled for this semester yet. Classes start in a couple weeks. I gotta decide what I'm doing about continuing in accounting or not."

"What are you waiting for?" she asked.

Lowering my voice, I leaned toward her and looked out the window to the parking lot.

"I guess I'm feeling a bit of a setback. And it's actually been a huge distraction." I saw a familiar car slowly pass by, and the temperature dropped twenty degrees inside me.

"Don't beat yourself up, sweetie," Jackie said, her

5

eyes glancing out the window but not seeing what I saw. "You've been through some shit. Do you think he's still looking for you?"

I shivered in the overheated restaurant as thoughts of my asshole ex-husband threatened to ruin my lunch.

"I want to believe he's not looking and that's he finally forgotten about me, but I'm not sure I'll ever get there. I could have sworn I saw his car the other day. I started shaking and froze right there in place. I need to be more resilient. Tougher. You know what I mean?"

Our food came, and I dove into my sandwich. At least I still had my appetite.

"Well, I'm sure you're just being paranoid. He'll never find you here. L.A.'s too big." Jackie watched a splotch of salad dressing land on her bosom, leaving an oily stain right on top of the girls. One of the downsides of having big ones?

I took a deep breath and looked at her, hoping to god she was right. I *needed* her to be right.

"So, that's what's been weighing on me. Now you know," I told her, deciding it was time to change the subject. "Hey, did I tell you the cutest guy came into the dealership the other day? He was so nice, chatting me up and all. Then Starla swept in and dragged him away."

"Ugh. She's such a whore."

The rivalry to end all others. I never should have brought her name up. No good would come of it.

And true to my fears, Jackie strung together a barrage of swear words that aptly conveyed her contempt for Starla. I got it—it was pretty much unheard of for a busy car dealership to have *one* top-selling woman, but to have *two* was freakishly uncommon. And those two went at it like pissed-off alley cats when the customers weren't around. The story was that when Jackie joined the company and started giving Starla a run for her money, all bets were off. Bigger screaming matches had never been seen or heard. Apparently the worst of it had been put to rest long before I'd joined the company—but their disdain for each other was barely concealed.

"Hey, we'd better get back," I said, checking the clock on the wall. "I don't want Ted yelling at me for being late. Again."

"That old windbag can suck my dick," Jackie said as she pulled out a twenty to cover our bill. She always paid at House of Waffles. I'd offer to pitch in or leave the tip, but she wouldn't allow me to. Like I could ever pay her back for all she'd done for me. Not in this lifetime.

Having something in common like abusive ex-husbands, as Jackie and I did, builds a serious bond between friends. We'd been thick as thieves ever since we learned each other's stories, and seriously had each other's backs.

She hooked her arm through mine as we walked back to her Mercedes.

"Ya know what, sweetie? I think you need a little nookie."

No shit. "I *know* I need a little nookie. Actually more than a little. But dontcha think I have bigger fish to fry at this point?"

Ignoring my prudence, she continued. "I may have an idea for you."

No, no, no. Jackie saying 'I may have an idea' was akin to someone saying 'hold my beer.' Disaster was usually the result.

"Jackie, I know all about your ideas. Thanks, but no thanks."

"Just give me a chance, Belle. You gotta trust me."

I smiled out the window. "You know what happened last time I trusted you."

"Hey, it wasn't my fault the guy used a fake picture on his profile," Jackie pleaded. "But he *did* pay for your drinks. So there's that."

I gave her the best stink eye I could muster.

"Miss Belle," Ted boomed.

Why was he hanging out behind the reception desk? *My* reception desk?

A quick look at my watch told me I was returning right on time. Not that it mattered. My backups in the service department always covered for me if I were late. 'Course, I did the same for them.

"Hi, Ted." I put on my headset and punched a few numbers on the phone console.

"Belle," he started, staring straight down at me in my chair.

Why did he have to be such a douchebag?

"I have a bone to pick with you," he continued.

Yeah, no shit, Sherlock.

"What's up, Ted? Is something the matter?" I asked with my best fake-pleasant voice.

"You didn't get me a very important phone message," he said in that imperious 'I'm the boss and I'm always correct' voice he used far too often.

"What? Are you sure?"

"Yes. A Mr. Reid called for me this morning. He's one of our best customers. Buys a new car for himself and nearly everyone in his family every year. He called me back just a few minutes ago, furious I'd not gotten back to him."

I turned to my computer and typed maniacally. I always entered online the messages I took and forwarded them to whoever was supposed to get them.

"There, Ted. Right there." I pointed at my screen that proved I had indeed sent him his message.

"Where? I don't see it. Where is it?" he asked, squinting through his glasses.

Dude needed to get his vision checked.

"Right there," I said, pressing my finger on the computer screen so he couldn't miss it.

9

"Oh," he said, snapping back up to his full height. "Well then."

Ah, the sweet taste of victory. "Is there anything else I can help you with, Ted?"

"No, Belle. There is not." He hurried back to his desk like his pants were on fire, while I just watched, shaking my head.

Christ, with men like him all over my ass, no wonder I'd not gone on a date in a year. Or had it been even longer?

And as if Ted's admonishment hadn't been humiliating enough, Starla happened by my desk.

"Hey'ya, Stella-Bella."

She thought we were good enough friends that she could nickname me.

"What's up, *Star*?" I asked.

"Oh, I hate that," she said, wincing. She leaned closer, like she wanted to girl gab with me.

"So how 'bout those new tits on Jackie? How much ya think she paid for them?"

"I really don't know, Starla. I didn't think to ask."

Of course I knew. Jackie had shared every last detail, even going so far as to ask my help on background checking the doctor. But that was between Jackie and me. Not Starla, who watched Jackie across the showroom work her magic on another bickering couple.

"Oh! Looks like my customer came back. Gotta go,"

she said, running as fast as she could in her six-inch stripper heels.

Finally, some peace. I pulled up the website for L.A. City College and found they still had room in their upcoming accounting classes. Could I pull this off another semester? I'd nearly killed myself last time, juggling school and work and trying to pay for the damn tuition. But if I didn't want to answer phones at Beverly Hills Motors for the rest of my life, I needed to get a degree in something more useful than art.

"Hey."

It was Jackie, and she'd scared the crap out of me.

"Damn. You okay?" she asked.

I lowered my voice and looked around. "I was checking out the class schedule at City College."

"Oh, awesome. Hey, I was thinking about your comment earlier today. I still want to help."

"What are you talking about?"

She cleared her throat and lowered her voice. "You know. About getting some."

She raised her eyebrows to make sure I was following..

When she was convinced I wasn't a total dolt, she continued. "There's this place. It's called The Agency." She held a white business card in her hand.

I reached for it, but she snapped it back.

"Give me a sec. I need to explain," she said. "If you call this place, the owner, Zenia, will help you, ya know, get back in the saddle." She finally handed over the card.

The only thing on it were the words *The Agency*, a website URL, and a local phone number.

All printed on some thick, high-quality card stock. Rich and creamy.

I flipped it over a few times in my fingers. "What is this? A dating service? Like Match.com?"

She looked around again, and only when she saw that the boss was on the other side of the showroom, did she continue. "No, that's not what it is. It's an... um...escort agency."

An escort agency... when Jackie said get back in the saddle, she wasn't joking.

"Oh. Well. Thanks. But I'm not interested in dating women. You know that's not my thing."

I pushed the card back toward her. She wouldn't take it.

"No, dummy," she said. I mean, I knew I needed to get some action. But *escorts*? "They don't have *female* escorts," she clarified. "They have *male* escorts."

No freaking way. How did a male escort service even exist? I mean, did women really hire...*dudes*?

"Well, I'm not sure that's the thing for me. And it's probably really expensive, anyway."

"You're right about that. It's not cheap. That's why I got you a gift certificate. I've already arranged it all with the owner, Zenia."

"You *what?*"

I looked around. Shit, I'd been loud, but the show-room was mostly empty, thank god.

"You *what*?" I repeated, whispering. "Why?"

She took a deep, patient breath. "Take the card home with you. Just think about it."

"I suppose you've done this before?" I asked.

She nodded and a huge smile spread across her face.

"Sure. Every now and then I want something a little different. The Agency always fits the bill. So to speak." She winked with great flair. "Oh, a customer. Gotta run."

She hustled across the showroom floor and out the door onto the lot, the smile never fading from her face.

CHAPTER 2

XANDER

Hell if I knew why I agreed to work out with Sandy. All he wanted to do half the time was flap his goddamn gums.

I put my weights down and glared at him as he finished complaining about the lack of 'tone' for his glutes. Seriously, not what I needed to listen to.

"I'm going to give you the straight talk about why you're not getting the results you want, San. You never shut up and actually do anything. It's that simple"

Sandy, The Agency's only gay escort, rolled his eyes. "What can I say, Xander? Not everyone likes working out like you do."

He looked me up and down, licking his lips. I didn't mind. I mean, I didn't play for his team, but hell, he *was* my friend. And his evaluation of the male body was dead-on. If Sandy liked the way a guy looked, you could bet all your money the female clients would, too.

Instead of arguing, he pointed to one of his tattooed triceps. "I'm not doing so bad. I mean, I'm hot, right?"

Dammit, he always somehow trapped me into giving him compliments. "You do look good, Sandy, for sure. I just thought you wanted to bulk up a bit."

He took a deep breath and sighed. "I do. I just didn't know it would be this hard." He put his hands on his hips and look around distastefully, as if the weights were dirty. "Seriously, how do you guys deal with all this...mass?"

Classic Sandy. Always unhappy with his lean body, but never wanting to do the 'dirty' work of gaining muscle.

Trying to set an example, I grabbed the dumbbell he found so offensive and started working my own bicep, raising and lowering it in the slow, even cadence of two up, four down. If he wanted to waste a workout, fine by me, but I was going to get my exercise on. I never missed a day.

He sank onto the weight bench opposite and watched my curls. You'd think he might do a few himself, since he was just sitting there. Instead, a giant smile spread across his face. "So, you have any interesting clients lately?"

It never failed. Time and again I'd tell him I didn't talk about my clients, and time and again, he'd come sniffing around for gossip. First off, it was against the rules to discuss clients, and our boss, Zenia, head of the agency, was all about rules. But second, it also seemed like an invasion of privacy. If I'd hired an escort for myself, I wouldn't want them talking about me. That shit was private. I wasn't a kiss-and-tell kind of guy, regardless of whether I was getting paid to spend time with a woman or not.

I had nothing but respect for my clients. All of them.

But I also knew if I didn't throw Sandy a bone, he'd never leave me the fuck alone.

So I caved. A little. "Yeah, San. I saw a librarian yesterday. She was pretty. All this hair piled on top of her head, big glasses. Curvy." I switched to a bigger set of dumbbells, really getting into the work, and hoping he'd just leave me alone.

"Aw c'mon, Xan, you never spill it. Did she suck your dick?"

"Oh, for Christ's sake." I let the weight hit the ground just next to Sandy's foot, causing him to almost jump out of his too-tight gym shorts.

"San, how many times have I told you, it's not cool to talk shit about clients?" I looked toward the door. Zenia was probably in her office scheduling appointments and all, but you never knew when she'd wander into the gym to say hi, maybe even to get some work in herself. No doubt about it, if she caught wind of his gossip, she'd put the kibosh on Sandy's big mouth in a New York minute.

He sniffed and folded his arms tight. "You don't have to be such a bitch about it,"

But his pout was short-lived. Unlike me, he didn't hesitate to dish about *his* clients. In fact, I was pretty sure he actually enjoyed it. He totally got off on knowing how many men wanted him.

"Well, since you didn't ask, I had an awesome client yesterday. He was a silver-fox kind of older man, know what I mean?" He shimmied his shoulders. "And I love me a silver fox. Something about a daddy complex..."

Ugh. There were some things about Sandy's work I just *didn't* want to hear the details of. I mean, how would he like it if I went on and on about how I loved pussy?

No, scratch that. He'd probably love it.

But it didn't matter. There was no shutting him up.

"Xander, you wouldn't believe it," he said, getting more excited by the minute. "Or maybe you would. We did this role-play thing where he was the boss and I was the security guard. I wore a uniform and everything. He wanted me to top him, like most of my dates do. Once they see what I'm packing, it turns even the biggest top into my bottom baby, and this one...oh honey, it was so fucking hot..."

I raised my voice to drown him out. "Sandy. You mind? Seriously, I don't need that shit right this second."

He rolled his eyes. "Ugh. You're so uptight. And you know, I can help you loosen up. Come play for my team sometime. A little walk on the wild side would do you good. Widen your horizons, so to speak. I know a couple of twinky bottoms who would have you singing *Trap Queen* by the time you're done."

Could someone please just shoot me, preferably in the head? I tuned him out and finished with the weights before beginning my transition to cardio. It wouldn't do to bulk up too much—I still had to fit into my designer clothes. There were a lot of demands on a modern-day escort, and fitting a role was one of them.

"Thanks, Sandy," I said to mollify his feelings and to keep him from staring at my crotch any more while I stretched. "If I wanted to be with a dude, believe me, you're the one I'd pick. But I probably never will. Just sayin'."

"I'll never give up on you, baby," he said with a shrug.

"Thanks, Sandy. I knew I could count on you."

Not content with his security guard story, he carried on. "Oh my god. I didn't tell you. Earlier in the week I had a date with a *couple*."

Oh cripes.

"Great. Happy for ya." I set myself up on the treadmill, hoping the machine's noise would drown him out.

No such luck. I seriously had to consider getting some headphones if this was going to continue. "This woman wanted to see her husband with another guy. Of course, when she called The Agency, Zenia right away said 'have I got the perfect guy for you.' So, this woman watched me and her husband get it on. It was pretty damn hot."

I was curious for once. "Did the woman try anything?"

He scrunched up his face. "She tried—little tongue action here and there on the ol' sack, but I kept redirecting her to her husband. She finally got the hint. I couldn't just outright shut her down, even though I would have liked to. I mean, that's what we get paid for, right?"

Sandy was the gayest gay man I'd ever known. I mean, some gay escorts would stomach being with a woman if it paid well, but not Sandy. He liked dick and that's all there was to it.

As the treadmill got up to speed and I felt the sweat really start to flow down my chest, the gym's door swung open. Our fellow escort, and Agency original employee, Richard, joined us. A bit of a 'silver fox,' Richard was also one of the biggest guys in the Agency, tipping the scales at a ripped two fifty of raw muscle. And he worked for it, too.

"Hey, guys." He slung a towel around his neck and adjusted the weights on the first machine in his rotation for the day, shoulder presses.

"Well, if it isn't Dick!" Sandy squealed. "It's a better day with Dick around!"

Richard closed his eyes and inhaled deeply. "Sandy. Nice to see you, too. And don't call me that."

"Oh, Richard. You know I love to tease. And may I say, you are looking *good*?"

"Thanks, San. You too. Hey, Xander. How's things?"

"Going good, man. Been busy. Zenia let me take some extra clients, so I'm getting some money in the bank. Building my nest egg in case my acting doesn't take off."

Richard smiled. "What? You want to leave all this behind?" He gestured around the room, two thousand square feet of private gym that was as well-equipped as any public club in LA. "But seriously, dude, good for you."

I had to hand it to Richard; he was always doing me a solid as one of my biggest supporters. He really believed in me when others were just naysayers.

There are too many actors in L.A.

You'll never make any money.

What do you know about show business?

I'd heard it all, and I didn't care. Someday I'd act, and I didn't mean in commercials. I meant *really act*. Besides, I couldn't escort forever, anyway. I mean, it was a good living and a lot of fun. I met some very nice ladies. But it wasn't a forever job. So I spent a good chunk of my free time and my money taking acting classes, doing improv shows, whatever I could to get miles under my belt, as one of my teachers called it.

"You're gonna make a fabulous movie star, Xander," Sandy said, watching Richard and me work up a sweat.

"Thank you, Sandy."

"Hey, Zenia says we have pretty full schedules for the next several weeks. As you can imagine, she's very happy about that," Richard said. "So you might want to take your ginseng and ginko pills with your shakes."

I liked that. And so did my bank account. I had plans, and the most important one was not to end up like my parents in dreadful military housing, moving from one base to another every two years of their lives. It had been my life, too, until I was old enough to get out.

"And how are you, Richard? And things at home?" I asked to pace myself. Fast enough to push out short bursts, not so slow I could just chat away.

He shrugged. "Same ol', same ol'."

"Rich, you are not still living with your mother, are you?" Sandy asked, rolling his eyes.

Richard adjusted his weight stack up a little higher. It was well known that he took care of his mother, who'd been laid up for almost as long as I'd known him.

"Yup. I am."

"Ugh. You gotta get out of there."

"Dude, I'm not going anywhere. She has dementia. She needs me."

"She still in the dark about your line of work?" I asked curiously. After all, how would you tell an eighty-two-year-old woman with dementia that her only son was an escort?

"Hell yeah. She doesn't need to know what I do. She thinks I'm a mailman. Problem is, she asks every mailman she sees if they know me."

"Oh, shit."

He hopped up from the shoulder-press machine, rolling out his arms as he came over. "It's kinda funny when you think about it, though. Here I am, escort extraordinaire, living with my elderly mother. Not very sexy at all. But no one knows that 'cept for you guys. Anyway, Xan, you fall in love with any clients lately?"

That cracked Sandy up.

"Hey, fuck you both. I have a lot of respect for my clients," I said.

They could be such asses.

Richard looked at Sandy, ignoring me. "Translation: *Xander falls in love easily.*"

"Whatever, guys." I dismounted my treadmill and rubbed a towel across my face. "Just because I respect them and not just their money doesn't mean I fall in love with them."

"Uh-huh... hey, I saw your American Express commercial the other day." Richard said.

"Seriously? They're still running that?" I asked, pleased. "Christ, I made that thing ages ago."

"What's up with the acting, anyway?" Sandy asked. "You still trying to make it on pure talent, or have you finally decided that the casting couch is your ticket to fame and fortune? You know, you could skip the waiting line—so to speak."

Richard rolled his eyes. "You're an asshole sometimes, Sandy, you know that?"

"Whatever, Rich. Xander has an adorable bubble butt. It's gonna make him famous. I mean, can't I say that if I want?"

I ignored him when he talked about my ass. Or any other body part, for that matter.

"It just so happens I have a couple auditions coming up for action-type martial arts roles."

Sandy screeched. Why? Because that's what he did.

"*Ohmygod*, I know you will get it. I just know!" He jumped up and down, clapping his hands. "You have to *promise—*"

A female voice interrupted, cutting through Sandy's excited screeching like a belt. "Excuse me, gentlemen."

We whipped around to find our beautiful benefactor, Zenia Porter, standing in the doorway, her nearly-six-foot-tall frame draped in a clingy black column of some designer garb I was sure had been ungodly expensive. Yup, she still had it in spades.

With the press of a button, my treadmill whirred to a stop, and Sandy and Richard leapt to their feet.

It wasn't that Zenia was foreboding or anything like that. In fact, she was warm and lovely, and had an easy laugh that could make you relax and feel good about your day no matter how shitty it had been. At least, when she *liked* you. And luckily for the three of us, she liked us. Of course, she made a lot of money off us. I never saw the Excel spreadsheet, even if there were one, but I bet we guys scored in her top five on a regular basis.

But what was unusual was that she seldom made in-person appearances. Most of the time we communicated with her, she was on the other end of a phone or text message. In fact, such long periods of time would go when we wouldn't see her that we'd begin to forget what she looked like, aside from being the tall, dark-skinned goddess that she was.

Rumor had it that when she was younger—in L.A., that meant any time before a woman hit her fortieth birthday—she was a marginally successful character actress. Meaning she wasn't famous enough for anyone to recognize her, but she worked steadily enough to make a good living. And when she reached her 'expiration date' and Hollywood was through with her, she funneled her cash into a venture more lucrative than any acting job she'd ever coveted.

Thus was born The Agency.

That's what she had named the company that first employed Richard, and later Sandy, me, and a handful of other guys, some of whom were her longtime lovers. The Agency was a company name so ambiguous—and yet serious—it took on any variety of meanings. It was whatever clients wanted it to be, by design.

"Zenia, good to see you," I said. And it was good to see her. She was even more beautiful than the last time I'd laid eyes on her. Some women, they hit a peak in their teens, some in their twenties or thirties. One in a million, though, are like Zenia, aging like fine wine.

"Xander, hello. And Richard and Sandy." She

elegantly acknowledged each of us with a nod. "I wanted to check in, say hi, see how everyone's doing." She clasped her hands, and without waiting for anyone to comment, continued. "We have a busy few weeks coming up. It's that time of year, and your regulars keep coming back. Better yet, I'm getting referrals for all of you, and new women are wanting to meet you. Except in your case, Sandy, it would be men."

Sandy fist-pumped the air. "Daddy do me right!"

Zenia looked away from him, trying not to laugh. She pampered Sandy when she could and tried to make sure that his clients would please him just as much as he pleased them.

"I just wanted to take a moment to reinforce that what The Agency offers is companionship. Nothing more, nothing less, both by Agency rules...and state law. As you know, that means you accompany your dates to events, dinner, on trips—anything they want and are able to pay for. Taking things to the next level —" she paused to look at each of us, one at a time, "—is up to you as consenting adults. The Agency neither condones nor condemns sexual activity between its employees and clients."

God, I loved that place. I could get laid. Or not. It was all up to me. Well, and my clients.

She continued. "This keeps The Agency above board, on the right side of the suits downtown, and out of trouble. I just like to restate this every now and again."

She turned for the door and stopped. "I've known you all for a good bit of time, especially you, Richard. Seems so long ago that we started. You're all loyal and hardworking, and I will never forget that. If the next few weeks go as well as I think they will, there will be nice bonuses in it for us all."

Yes.

Needless to say, we were all smiles. We couldn't wait to get to work.

Who could blame us?

CHAPTER 3

BELLE

In the dingy hallway in the back of House of Waffles where the bathrooms were housed, there was an ancient pay phone on the wall.

And by all great miracles, it also *worked*.

It might sound strange, but I knew this hallway well. Better than I wanted to, that was for sure. I'd memorized the graffiti on the wall by the men's room door, where the cracks in the linoleum-tiled floor fell under my feel, and how the sour odor of an empty milk crate would sting my nose until I didn't notice it anymore.

I'd spent a good deal of time in that crappy little hallway, using what was probably the last operational pay phone in L.A., making phone calls I couldn't risk being traced. Which was pretty much anytime I had to call back at home to West Virginia, or speak to someone who might be connected to my ex-husband.

My call was answered on the first ring. "Hello?"

The familiar voice on the other end of the line stirred a mix of comfort for its familiarity, and sadness that I might never hear it in person again.

"Nina." I had to fight the growing lump in my throat. It had been too long since I'd seen the woman who had grown up with me as my best friend. We'd swapped stories of first dates, first kisses, and first heartbreaks. She'd saved my life more than she ever knew, and when she slipped that extra two hundred into my hand one day, it was the only way she knew to say goodbye. But I still kept in touch when I could.

"Oh my god, Belle," Nina said, the accent still so strong and so missed it brought tears to my eyes. There was something comfortable in that coal-country twang. "It's good to hear your voice. How are you, sweetie?"

"I'm well, Nina." I took a deep breath and nodded to myself. "Yeah, I'm good."

"Is everything okay? Are you gonna tell us where you are?" she asked. "God, I want to at least send you a Christmas card or something!"

"I can't, Nina. I'm sorry. It's not safe yet."

"I understand, hon."

"Have you seen him?" I held my breath.

"No. But I asked about him recently, and they said

he'd gone down to the Caribbean for a vacation. With a new woman."

My breath caught. If he was with someone new, that would mean he was done with me. Right?

"I never thought I'd be so happy to hear Todd Thomas was off with another woman." I laughed a little too hard, unsure whether I was just blowing off steam or if it really was funny that Todd had someone new.

"I hope you come home soon, Belle," Nina said.

I got it. We were from one of those towns where people left and didn't come back. Even when they weren't fleeing a living hell of a marriage.

"Everyone asks about you."

"You tell them what I told you, right?" I ask, suddenly worried. One slip, that's all it would take.

"Sure do, sweetie," Nina reassured me. "I've not heard hide nor hair of you. I'm such a good actress, I should get an Academy Award. They buy it every time, hook, line, and sinker."

"Okay. Good. Thank you. I'll call you next week. Same time?"

"Sounds good." She lowered her voice. "Okay. I gotta run. Dan and the kids are home. I don't want them asking questions."

"All right. Bye, Nina. Thank you for everything. Love you."

"Love you, too, sweetie."

And she was gone.

As much as my new life in L.A. was coming

together, I'd be lying if I didn't admit to being a little homesick for the West Virginia town I'd lived in all my life, until the day I couldn't be there anymore.

"Good morning, sir. Welcome to Beverly Hills Motors." I popped off my stool to greet a man so handsome my heart was pounding in my ears.

And then he smiled at me. "Hello. I was wanting to talk to someone about one of your sports coupes."

Before I could answer, because, let's be honest, I was stunned by his glittering dark eyes and incredible chin dimple, our exchange was interrupted.

"Hello. I'd *love* to help you today." Jackie extended her hand and somehow managed to maneuver her new tits right into the guy's line of sight.

"How do you do?" He took her hand.

"Why don't you come this way with me?" she offered, leading him across the room to a comfy little seating area she called 'her office.'

I thought maybe he'd look back over his shoulder at me.

He didn't.

Taking it as a sign from fate that this guy was not my type, I settled back onto my stool to answer the ringing phones and to replay in my head the Waffle House pay phone chat I'd had with Nina.

I wasn't sure whether to be glad that Todd had a new woman—or to be broken-hearted that the man I'd loved since high school had turned out to be such a fucker.

And a crazy fucker he was, too, who'd hurt me so badly I had to leave town with no trace, looking over my shoulder every minute of every day. Even now, if a doctor looked at my X-rays, they could find the evidence of how Todd 'consummated' our marriage. He just needed to know where to look.

Could that ugly, destructive fear that had caged and defined me for so long finally be gotten rid of? It seemed too good to be true.

"Hey, girl."

Before I snapped my head up, I knew it was Starla. She and Jackie had been trading acidic barbs back and forth all day. But hey, she'd done nothing to me, so I wasn't going to be a shit to her just for Jackie's sake. I had to be neutral in their little kitty war.

Probably the main thing that bugged me about Starla was that when she happened by the reception desk looking for someone to chat up, her perfume arrived before she did. And it was not the good kind of perfume. She honestly smelled like an exploded perfume department where she'd been doused with everything at once. I didn't see how customers could do test-drives with her, with that fragrance sucking all the air out of the car.

"How's your day going, Starla?" I asked.

It was actually nice to have a distraction, given what I'd been obsessing over.

She gestured across the showroom with her chin. "Hey, you see that guy over there, who Jackie's sucking up to? The tall, good-looking one?"

"Yes, I see him."

Of course I'd seen him—did she think I was blind? I mean, after all, he'd spoken to me when he'd first arrived.

She snorted so loudly, heads in the showroom turned in our direction. "His kid's in preschool with my daughter. I fucked him after the last PTA meeting."

No, no, no. Please spare me...

"Yeah, his dick's so big, I could hardly walk the next day—"

I held my hand up. There were lines to cross, and lines not to cross. She just didn't know the difference. "Starla, that's enough. I really don't want to hear about who you were or were not with, and what you did with them."

"Right. Sorry. Forgot you weren't into that sort of chitchat. I'll never learn, will I?" Her gaze wandered across the showroom as she looked for a new victim to share her sexcapades with, but she wasn't done with me just yet. "So what about you?" she asked as she looked me up and down.

"What about me?"

"You getting any? You've been here long enough now to have caught someone's fancy. A pretty, classy girl like you. And you've got that soft twang that I know drives the guys wild. I've faked one myself often enough, more Alabama southern than West Virginia, but out here in L.A., they don't know any different. So c'mon. Who are you hooking up with?"

"No one, Starla."

I wasn't sure I even wanted to be with a guy again, Jackie's offer of a male escort notwithstanding.

She looked me up and down. "You know, if you got some new tits like Jackie did, that might open some doors for you. Man-wise."

Did she really just say that? Seriously, with all I had to deal with and the crap I put up with at my job, she tosses off the suggestions of plastic surgery?

It was all so L.A.

I smiled brightly. "Thank you, Starla. I can always count on your unfiltered opinion."

My snarkiness was lost on her. "Sure thing, Belle. Any time."

As soon as she wandered off in her too-tight skirt and too-high heels, I opened the LA. City College website, and finally registered for my accounting class. No more screwing around—I was going to finish this degree. No more waiting around for all of life's dominoes to line up perfectly. Setting myself up for success was not the sort of thing that could wait, and if I had to wing it, then that's how it would be.

~

A little later, while checking my pockets for a buck to get a soda with, I pulled the card Jackie had given me out of my pocket.

The one that said *The Agency*.

On the other side of the showroom, she was still working her customer, the super-handsome man, by running a finger up his arm while showing him how to open the top on a convertible. If I knew her at all, she'd take him for a drink after they'd struck a deal. And go home together after that. Who knew car dealerships were such hotbeds for hookups?

Ted, on the other side of the floor, was wheeling and dealing with a mother-daughter duo who were practically identical twins. Long blonde hair, flawless skin, in what looked like very expensive leather jackets. Part of me was jealous of the mom for looking so young, the other jealous of the girl, knowing she had the genes to still look that good when she was on the north side of forty. I overheard them saying they wanted matching cars. Typical Beverly Hills. And knowing Ted, he'd be making the moves on one if not both of them before they'd left.

L.A. was teeming with sexiness. And it seemed like everyone was getting laid.

Everyone, except for me.

For the longest time, sex had been the *last* thing on my mind. Every bit of emotional energy I had was sucked up by the pain of what turned out to be the last straw in my marriage. While I remembered, I ran my finger over the scar on my temple, like I did a hundred times a day, where Todd had nearly blinded me by smacking me with a picture frame.

A picture frame containing a beaming image of us the day we got married.

That's when I knew it was over. Actually, truth be told, maybe we never even got started. Stars in your eyes will blind you to a lot of things, and I was one of those kinds of women, raised in one of those kinds of towns where things happened. In L.A., if a man laid a finger on a woman, she had the law on her side. Back home...it was different. But for some reason, the picture frame did what the other injuries couldn't—like force me to realize if I didn't get out, my life would be cut short. But I wasn't going to be one of those kinds of women any longer.

Convinced everyone else in the dealership was occupied and would be for a while, I tapped on my keyboard and ended up on The Agency's website. It was sleek and simple, just like the business card Jackie had given me. And like the business card, it barely revealed anything, other than the 'companionship' it professed to offer.

"Belle! Whatcha doin'?"

My heart just about burst out of my chest. I turned to see one of my coworkers from the service depart-ment, a nice enough guy named Sam, looking over my shoulder.

"What's that?" Sam asked, pointing at my monitor,

which I closed as fast as I could. "Some sort of fancy spa or something?"

"Yes. That's exactly what it is," I lied, hoping he would buy it. "I've got a friend with a birthday coming up. I was thinking a gift certificate or something would be nice."

"It looks super-expensive," he continued, moving to see the screen I was blocking with my shoulder. "You sure are a good friend."

"Things busy over in Service?" I clicked the page closed, praying that Jackie never got wind of my nearly being caught. She'd tease me incessantly if she did.

He shrugged. "Not too bad. Just thought I'd stretch my legs. Hey, I'm going out for a Starbucks. Want anything?"

"Oh, thank you. No, I'm good."

"All right, Belle. Just don't let me see you drinking that shitty stuff they call coffee in the customer waiting room. That'll kill ya…"

He wandered off, waving behind himself as he pushed open the side door and adjusted the ball cap on his head.

Holy shit. Close call.

I didn't dare re-open The Agency's web page. I couldn't risk it. But before I'd closed it, I had seen one thing of interest.

Deep-tissue massage.

I wasn't sure what that was, but it sounded

awesome, and if Jackie was picking up the bill, why the hell not?

At home that night, I pulled out The Agency's card once again.

Christ, I was a wuss.

I laid it on my nightstand as I crawled into bed, and flipped open my iPad—a gift from Jackie for watching her kids for a weekend. If there were ever nominations for patron saints of best friends, Jackie's name would be front and center.

My dear, dear Jackie. Just before I'd left work that day, she'd cornered me and asked if I'd given any thought to The Agency. I told her I hadn't gotten to it yet. But because she seemed to have taken an interest in my sex life, she also told me about a website called YouPorn.

"What is that? Like YouTube?" I'd asked.

"Well, I guess, sort of. People post videos, but they're of sex. You know, fucking."

Was she for real?

"Jackie, I know what sex is. You don't have to define it for me."

"It's really cool. Every night, after the kids are asleep, I get in bed with my vibrator—"

I held my *stop sign* hand. "I don't want to know what you do with your vibrator, Jackie."

But she was not deterred. She never was.

"—and I pull up YouPorn. They have some hot shit on there. Gay, straight, lesbos, interracial, you name it—"

"Okay, okay, Jackie. I get the picture."

Satisfied she'd gotten her point across, she smiled.

"Cool, babe. Hey, I see a new customer coming in."

Before I could even take two breaths, she was off to make another deal. That customer might have come in just to look, but when Jackie was through with her, she'd be walking out with a brand-spanking-new car.

That's why she was number one.

And that's how I ended watching YouPorn.

When I powered up my iPad, I got the vibrator going, too. Which, as you may have guessed, was another gift from Jackie.

I flipped through the videos, and holy shit, there was a lot to choose from. And anal. So much anal. Not that that was my thing. I mean, I'd never tried it. Actually hadn't tried much of anything. That's how things went down when you married your 'high school sweetheart' and never got to go through the slut phase so many of my friends did.

At the time, I'd told myself it was okay. I was at home watching *Jeopardy* with my new husband, Todd, while my friends were out having fun.

I'd only ever had sex with him and one other guy, but Todd had always told me I sucked in bed. So I didn't try much with him.

I mean, why bother? Safer that way—just let him get his rocks off, roll over in bed, and start snoring.

But if I could learn accounting, I could also learn to be better in the sack. I clicked *start* on a YouPorn vid that had a nice thing going with two women and one guy. One of them was sitting on his face and the other was giving him a blowjob.

I turned my vibe on *low* and ran it up and down my slit. The guy in the vid had shifted everyone around and was now doing one of the women from behind, who was bent down with her face between the thighs of the other. They seemed to be having smashing time, but who knew? They were porn actors, right?

Regardless of whether they actually *were* having the time of their lives, I knew I was enjoying the hell out of watching them. I ran my vibe over my hard-as-a-rock clit, and just as the blonde being fucked from behind started to howl, my legs began to quiver. What started as a tickle legs erupted into a full-on explosion of the nuclear kind as my own moans drowned out three porn stars. I didn't even know I could do that. I lost my grip on my iPad, and it and my *YouPorn* friends tumbled to the floor with a *thud*. I turned over to ride the vibrator to another orgasm that left me screaming, "Fuck, fuck, fuck!"

It ended all too quickly when a knock on the wall scared the shit out of me.

"Quiet down! Some of us are trying to get some sleep over here, you pervert!" came through the thin wall separating my bed from someone who I was apparently keeping awake.

Shit. Just when I start having fun, I get busted for too much noise.

Just my goddamn luck.

CHAPTER 4

BELLE

S top it.

Just stop being so chickenshit and park the damn car.

I'd driven around the block three times, scoping out The Agency. It wasn't that I couldn't find a parking spot. That was the least of my worries, actually. The building was nice, in a part of town that I wouldn't have thought would hold an escort service—not that I knew what part of town *would*. It was just that I couldn't decide whether or not to go inside. I was simply frozen behind the wheel of my little car, circling the block on autopilot.

But Jackie's voice echoed through my thoughts. She'd set up a meeting for me with the woman who was the owner. I *had* to go in. If I didn't, I'd never hear the end of it.

Park the damn car.

So I did, and after sitting for a couple of minutes and wondering if the black sheath dress I'd worn was the right choice, I reached into the back seat for my shoes. I kicked off the flip-flops I'd driven in and began the task of buckling up the skyscraper heels I got at DSW. I hadn't dared to drive with them on—L.A. traffic was scary enough as it was. So I locked the doors to my VW Bug and mincingly walked toward a beautiful storefront with a striped awning, wondering why I'd worn the damn heels. Seriously, who was I trying to impress?

The Agency looked more like a law office than anything else, not entirely out of place on the chic and trendy Melrose Avenue. The famous Fred Segal boutique in all its glory was just a few doors down, where movie stars poured in and out all day with bagsful of the latest fashions.

The front door was locked. Of course. You couldn't have just anyone wandering into...whatever the place was supposed to be. A few seconds of searching revealed the hidden doorbell, so I pressed it, while part of me hoped no one would answer.

No such luck.

"Hello. You must be Belle. I'm Zenia."

One of the most stunning women I'd ever seen had pulled open the door. She must have been nearly six feet tall in her heels, with dark brown skin and eyes that glittered from behind cat's-eye glasses. And the strange thing was, she looked vaguely familiar.

But I couldn't possibly know her. I knew very few people in L.A. I preferred to keep a low profile that way.

I extended my hand, hoping she wouldn't notice it shaking. "Hi. Nice to meet you."

"Let's go up to my office, shall we?" she suggested with a smile.

I hoped she'd have a place to sit, because I thought I might faint if I had to stand for long.

But I needn't have worried. Zenia's office was more than just a place to sit. I settled into a velvet chair opposite her desk and scanned the room. Her office had a modern-y, Zen-y feel to it with a row of bamboo stalks shielding the windows from the afternoon sun, and a large glass Buddha statue over looking it all. It was spotless, with every surface gleaming mellowly, as soft music played from invisible speakers. It even smelled nice. Kind of spicy, like expensive essential oils.

Clasping her hands, she leaned forward on her desk.

"Can I get you something to drink, Belle? Some tea?"

"Oh, that would be great. Thank you."

Anything to stall and put off the inevitable conversation. I didn't know what to expect, but I was petrified.

Would she want to know how many sexual partners I'd had? Whether I'd done threesomes or moresomes? Whether I had any decent underwear? Actually, I did. Nothing high-end, but it was clean and pretty, and from the Victoria's Secret sale bin.

While she busied herself with the tea, she spoke over her shoulder.

"How did you find us, Belle?"

"One of my friends told me about you. Do you know—"

Shit. Had Jackie told me not to give out her name? I couldn't remember.

She set the steaming teacups down and put a bowl with sugar cubes between us. I reached for two and stirred them into my tea. Thank god I had another place to look other than her beautiful, inquiring face.

Zenia seemed to have noticed my reluctance to say Jackie's name and hummed in appreciation. "That's okay, Belle. You don't have to tell me who sent you. It's actually quite a compliment to your friend that you are so…discreet."

I looked back up at her. She seemed so *nice*.

"What can we do for you today?" she asked.

I squirmed in my seat because, of course.

"Well, um, I'm coming off of a bad divorce..." I started before my words trailed off. Finally, I cleared my throat. "Really bad."

"I'm sorry to hear that. We see a lot of women coming out of divorces. They want to get back up on the horse, so to speak."

She had a small smile on her face, which I tried to mimic. Not so sure I succeeded.

"Right. So, my friend J—" I stopped myself. "My friend treated me to...um...your agency's services."

"What a nice friend. You two must be very close."

Was a friend who told you about vibrators and porn sites a close friend? I'd say so. About the only way she could get closer would be if she gave me demonstrations, and that was just not going to happen.

"Let me tell you a bit about how we work here at The Agency, Belle," Zenia continued. "We offer massage and companionship only. Any sexual contact must take place outside the agreement you have with us."

Um. Yeah, right. I'm sure all escort services said the same thing in L.A.

"Do you understand that, Belle?" She was studying me, and my heart stopped for a moment.

Shit, did she think I was a cop?

"Yes, I understand, Zenia. Sounds good. And a massage sounds wonderful. Just what I need," I said.

She opened a drawer and pulled out a tiny laptop

that she typed a couple things into. "Very good. Then let me see…"

My mind whirled while she worked. I still had time to bolt. Maybe the money Jackie had given me could be better spent on something else.

Like new tires for my car.

Oh, and my tuition bill would be coming due.

But if I didn't get something going with a guy, even if he were a hired hand, Jackie would never let me hear the end of it. Maybe I could have him over my apartment to clean…

I could always lie and tell Jackie I'd gotten the best nookie of my life. It's not like she'd ask for proof.

"Belle? Belle? Are you okay?"

I snapped up, realizing I'd been spacing. "Sorry. Wandering mind."

She smiled brightly and turned her laptop so I could see the screen.

"I understand. Now, for the fun part. As you can see, we have a number of gentlemen for you to choose from."

Holy. Shit.

I reached to pull the laptop closer as the room suddenly grew warmer. The guys I was looking at were not mere mortals. It just wasn't possible, unless someone had gone crazy with Photoshop. Before me were the kind of men you looked at from across the room and *wished* would talk to you, but you knew never would. The kind how, when you're a kid, you sign your name a hundred times practicing as if you were married and had their last name. The kind of guys who walked into a restaurant and people stopped talking. The kind of guys created by the universe on a *good* day, when there wasn't a single mistake made in anyone's DNA. Not even one oversized pore on their face.

The kind of guys who weren't into *me*.

I pushed the laptop back.

"Do you have another level down? I mean, I don't think these are my kind of guys."

Zenia's eyebrows rose. "What do you mean?"

I shook my head. "They're way too good-looking for me."

She looked puzzled. "Belle. Do you not know how beautiful you are?"

Okay. What was this woman smoking?

"Thank you, Zenia. It's just that, you know. I thought you might have different guys to choose from. You know, like a regular guy."

She pushed the laptop aside and leaned on the desk again.

"Tell me, Belle. What do you like in a man?"

"Um. Well, I'm not sure."

"How many men have you been with?" she continued, undeterred. "I mean intimately."

She did *not* just ask me that question.

She waited. Patiently.

"One," I mumbled.

"Excuse me?"

I cleared my throat. No sense in lying, and no sense in being embarrassed.

"Two. My ex-husband and one other fling I had in college."

She typed something in her computer. Shit. Now my lame sexual background was part of a permanent record.

"That's nothing to be ashamed of. We have some women in here who are virgins, looking for their first experience."

"Well I'm not that bad off—"

Oops. From the look of her stink-eye, I needed to keep my big mouth shut.

She sighed and went back to tap-tapping on her keyboard.

"We try not to judge," she said without looking up, but not unkindly. "The Agency exists to help our clients, regardless of their background or tastes... within reason, of course."

"Right. Sorry. I didn't mean anything by it."

Was she going to kick me out now? Maybe that wouldn't be such a bad thing...Jackie couldn't argue with that...

"So Belle. What do you like? Hairy chest or no hairy chest? Big cock or small cock?"

Wait.

Did she just say something about *cocks*?

She must have, because she sat there, fingers poised

over her keyboard, like she was waiting for the most important piece of information I could possibly provide.

"Um. I don't know," I mumbled. I mean, I'd only had two—what did I know about cock size?

She typed another couple things, and turned the laptop to face me again.

"Could you scroll through these men here? Tell me if you see anyone you like?"

I ran my finger across the screen and found that each man was more handsome than the last. These pictures must have been doctored up. I knew L.A. was full of good-looking people, but this many gorgeous men in one place? Nah. I turned the computer back to Zenia. Time to have some balls. So to speak.

"I'm not sure the size of someone's...cock...is that important. I'd rather have someone *nice.*"

Her face seemed to relax, and even a hint of a smile came out on her face.

"Okay. That's very helpful. I know the perfect man for you. His name is Xander Johnson. As sweet at they come."

She spun the laptop around again.

Oh. *Oh.*

Zenia's Mr. Johnson was gorgeous in a blond, preppy, boy-next-door sort of way. Blue eyes looking right into the camera.

Damn.

"Um. Yeah. He'd be good, Zenia. Yes. I'll take him."

I felt like I was grocery shopping.

"Super!" she said.

"You think he'll, um, be okay with me? I mean, guys like that do not date girls like me."

I know that sounded pathetic, but she already knew how lame I was, so what was the harm in her knowing more?

And I guess she took my question seriously, because she got up, came around the front of her desk, and propped her butt on the corner of it to lean toward me.

"When you get home, I want you to look in the mirror and do something for me. Take two minutes, close your eyes, and then open them. Open them and look at how lovely you really are, Belle. I don't know how Xander will keep from falling in love with you."

I burst out laughing. I couldn't help it.

"What's so funny, Belle?"

I took a deep breath. "Life has been a little crazy. I left a terrible, abusive marriage. See this scar here?"

I pointed to what was by now a long, thin white mark that ran the length of my temple.

"Good lord, sweetie," Zenia said, tracing the mark with a warm fingertip. "That's terrible."

I nodded. It was all I could manage. Zenia's kind words had me all choked up. She reached for my hand. "You're going to be okay, Belle. And you'll like Xander. I promise you, when I say sweet, he truly is. He's kind, intelligent...and no, I'm not just talking him up. He's one of the best 'nice guys' you'll ever meet."

Whoa. I hadn't even met him, and I was already swooning. "Well, even if I don't like him, he'd be no worse than my ex."

"Where is your ex, now?" Zenia asked.

"I think he's on vacation. With another woman."

She refilled my tea. "Does he know where you are?"

My head snapped in her direction as the hairs on the back of my neck stood up in alarm.

"No. At least I hope to god he doesn't know. If he did find me…well, I'm not sure what he'd do."

That's why I was three thousand miles away from him, and no one in my hometown knew where I was.

"Well, Belle, I've been in L.A. for a long time. I know a lot of people. If there is ever anything I can do to help, I hope you'll let me know."

Relief flooded through me, and I nodded gratefully. "Thank you, Zenia. You've already done more than you can imagine."

CHAPTER 5

XANDER

Coming out of the studio lot, I pumped my fist, resisting the urge to beat my chest and holler in excitement.

I'd just nailed an audition. At least it felt that way.

I wasn't that great at auditions. For the longest time, they held me back. But I'd been on so many, I'd gotten to the point where I could handle them without freaking the hell out. I was getting to be a champ at hiding the bag of nerves I was every time I read for a movie.

To say I wanted the role I'd just auditioned for was an understatement—I wanted it *bad*. I'd get to use my martial arts background and maybe even work with Arnold Schwarzenegger. Not on camera of course—the man was over seventy—but he was an executive producer and would be around the set on a regular basis.

That would *seriously* be the shit.

And if I didn't get it—well, there would be others. There would always be others.

I couldn't complain. Zenia and The Agency took good care of me. I got the best clients a guy in my line of work could hope for. No, they didn't all look like supermodels. In fact, they rarely looked like any kind of model at all. But there was something profoundly beautiful about each woman I spent time with, regardless of whether all we did was go to a gallery opening and have a glass of wine, or if I spent hours in bed with her, making her feel like she never had before.

In some ways, The Agency had prepared me to be a better actor. It allowed me to find that spot in a character, to find that connection, and really immerse myself in the mind of what I was reading for. Just like I did on a date with a client. I'd identify what a woman needed most and make her feel like the most beautiful, desirable, precious thing in the world. More than once, I would keep that image with me for days afterward. It was why Sandy and Richard teased me about falling for my clients.

Yeah, I had a damn good life.

And pretty far from what I'd been destined for.

My dad had been career Army. We'd moved all over, always living in shitty military-base housing and going to shitty base schools filled with more juvenile delinquents than anything else. Pretty ironic that the kids of military families were so often such a mess.

I got out of there the first chance I got. And I never looked back.

My parents had been shocked I'd not wanted to go into the military. All my brothers had. My sister married a guy in the military. But me, I knew there had to be more out there. The day after I graduated from high school, I got on a Greyhound in Alabama that dropped me at a grimy bus station in downtown L.A. Within hours, I'd found a place to stay with a bunch of other guys, and a job valet parking cars.

Those were fun days, I couldn't deny it. I wasn't making much money, but the memories were great. Still, I wouldn't trade my life now for anything.

Speaking of my first L.A. job, I pulled up to the swanky Roosevelt Hotel and tossed my keys to the kid parking cars, pressing a twenty into his palm to take extra-good care of my ride. I was running late due to the audition I'd just finished, but I wiped my sweaty brow with a hanky, smoothed the wrinkles out of my Armani suit, and headed for the bar to find my date for the evening.

I looked around the hotel lobby that screamed money and elegance. I was a long way from home, no doubt about that.

Zenia had briefed me on the woman I was to meet. She'd said she seemed a little fragile and could use some special sweetness. In my experience, every woman had a bit of a fragile side—I guess that's what I loved about them. It didn't matter to me—big or small, young or old—I pretty much adored them all.

And the other guys loved to give me shit about it.

I'd fallen into escorting by accident. Zenia had seen me working the valet stand at TheStandard Hotel downtown and had given me her number. Told me she wanted to talk to me about some work.

At first I thought she was hitting on me. I was honestly flattered, even if she was a 'cougar' by my standards, but she was legit in her offer of work. The rest was history. She taught me how to be a gentleman, how to dress, how to treat a lady, and even how to properly make love. Yup, Zenia tested all her guys before she let them loose on clients, and I'd cherish those lessons for the rest of my life. I think all of her escorts did. Well, except for Sandy. Still, I'd be lying if I didn't say all us guys had a bit of a crush on her. Maybe even Sandy did, too, just in a different way.

The hotel's bar was stylishly dim, and I waited in the doorway while my eyes adjusted to the low light. There was one woman at the bar, and she was wearing the small red flower in her hair that Zenia had all new clients wear as a signal to their escort.

Belle Thomas.

Zenia hadn't told me anything more about her. She preferred for us to learn and react as we went. She did say she was very pretty.

What she didn't say was that she was fucking beautiful.

I'd be lying if I didn't feel a bit of a twitch in my trousers.

I wasn't usually a stalker, but there was something about this woman that grabbed me, and I wanted to watch her before she became aware of my presence. From where I stood, I saw she had a slim build and long blonde hair. Couldn't complain about that. But the way she held herself, just sitting on a stool at a fancy bar with her hand on a glass of white wine, spoke volumes. Her posture was straight, and she struck me as someone who had truly found what it meant to be strong, to respect herself, and though she might see life as a work in progress, she was finding her way there. It made her graceful. Elegant. Comfortable in her skin.

I needed to know more.

"May I help you, sir?"

A rail-thin hostess had noiselessly floated up next to me and caught me spying. A typical L.A. girl. I'd probably seen her at one of the cattle-call auditions, but just in passing.

"I'm meeting a friend. She's over there."

"Wonderful, sir. Let me bring you to her. She's been waiting only a few minutes," she said, leading me over. As she approached the bar, she cleared her throat. "Miss, your friend is here."

Belle whipped around, and damn if she didn't have the most amazing light brown eyes I'd ever seen.

I leaned in to kiss her cheek at the same time she extended her hand for a shake and we crashed into each other, leaving the hostess smiling. She probably saw shit like that all the time. First dates, meeting in a fancy bar. This was L.A. life and L.A. dating.

Just like Belle and me. Except we weren't really dates. Not exactly.

So I took her hand, firm and warm, not like some of those women who shake with their fingertips and just let their wrists go limp. No, she had a background that said she knew a real handshake and wouldn't hide it either. It was sexy, as sexy as her supple lips and enchanting eyes. As we parted, I went for another attempt at a kiss, this time succeeding.

"Nice to meet you, Belle. I'm Xander."

For a moment I wondered if she could speak—she just stared at me with an adorable crooked smile.

"Um. Hi." Her words came out croaky, but even in the two she spoke, there was a hint of an accent, and in my trousers things moved again.

"Mind if I grab this seat, Belle?" I wanted her to feel in control. She'd hired *me*, after all.

But the truth was I'd be directing the evening, just like I always did. Women didn't hire an escort to hang out with some wimp. They wanted a tough-as-nails alpha, and I always delivered, but in my own way.

She took a deep breath. Smart girl. That always helped with the nerves. "Hi, Xander. Yes, please have a seat."

"What can I get you, sir?" the bartender asked.

I never broke eye contact with Belle and answered the man without turning my head. "Scotch and soda, please. And Belle, are you ready for something else?"

"Sure. I'll have another chardonnay."

"Coming right up." He left two small menus in front of us.

"This place has great small plates, if you'd like something," I said, trying to assess what she was up for.

It wasn't always easy to gauge what a client wanted so early in the evening. And yet, that's what made us guys at The Agency so good at what we did. A few subtle hints, and we knew where to take things and when. It all came down to timing and eventually became like a sixth sense for us. I mean, if you didn't pick it up, your clients didn't come back and Zenia didn't keep you around.

Nothing personal in that regard. It was just business.

And Belle was studying her bar menu like it was a textbook. So, I picked up mine, flagged down the bartender, and ordered olives and nuts.

I'd normally follow my client's lead when it came to conversation. First, they'd ask me where I was from, typically, which would open the door for me to ask a few questions and get them to open up about themselves.

But at that moment in time, Belle seemed more interested in her menu than me or anything else. But I didn't take it personally. She was nervous, no doubt. I was there to help.

"Mind if I try a sip of your wine, Belle? I never drink chardonnay."

She looked surprised. But that was a good thing. Snap her out of her embarrassment, or whatever it was she was struggling with.

"Um, sure." She pushed her glass toward me.

I took a sip. And grimaced. "Yeah, I just don't think white wine is my thing."

She laughed. It was a soft, country laugh, not Southern but not Western either. There was something musical to it, and I had my opening into some casual conversation.

I seized my moment.

"What kind of work do you do?" I asked.

"I am a receptionist at Beverly Hills Motors. But I'm also taking classes. Accounting classes."

"All right. Good for you. Ambition." I raised my scotch, and she met my glass with her wine.

"Absolutely," she agreed.

"Are you from L.A.?" I asked leadingly, mostly to see where her background was.

"Oh, no. I'm from the East Coast. Been out here a year or so."

She looked down at her wineglass, and I was curious. Most people, most clients, were more than happy to spill about their hometown, whether it was the mock embarrassed 'aw shucks, it's this little town you've never heard of,' to the brassy 'Lower East Side, dontcha know?'

Not Belle. I wasn't sure whether to probe, but I also knew she'd let me know how much she wanted to share.

"What brought you out here?"

She tensed up. Shit. I should have asked something else.

She took a deep breath summoning from some inner well of courage. "Bad divorce. You know how that goes."

"Oh yeah," I replied, feeling lame even as I say it. Nothing Zenia or any of the other guys had taught me helped with that particular topic, other than to plunge in and get it over with quickly. "The divorce club is a big one. No one really wants to join it, but it happens."

"What about you, Xander? Where are you from?" she asked, and I let out an inner sigh, glad that part was over.

"I was an Army brat. Grew up all over, but mostly in the South. I couldn't wait to get out. Came to L.A. first chance I got."

"How has it worked out for you? I mean, do you like being a…an escort?"

Ah. There it was. All women wanted an answer to that question.

"I meet awesome people from all walks of life. So yes, I would say I like it very much."

"How many of them do you sleep with?" she asked.

Damn. She was pulling no punches.

"You might be surprised. Very few of them, actually. Most times, we're hired to accompany someone to an event or just go to a nice dinner. I do quite a lot of my work as a plus one for weddings, conventions, stuff like that."

"Oh," she said, sounding very relieved. "Interesting."

"And we can do whatever you're comfortable with, Belle. But I do want to tell you something."

Alarm crossed her face. "What? Is something wrong?"

"No. I don't think anything is wrong at all."

"Oh. Okay," she said.

I leaned in, inhaling her scent and savoring it, letting it sear its way into my mind and letting me slip further into being her man for the night. "I wanted to tell you that, regardless of what you think, you're stunningly beautiful."

"Oh. Oh. Well, thank you." She blushed, truly surprised at my compliment.

Her reaction was cute as hell and made my dick hard even as part of me grew angry inside. She was divorced, and it seemed her ex never told her she was beautiful? Good riddance to the fucker. I fingered a strand of hair hanging down the front of her simple black dress and noticed a long, thin scar on her temple. Probably from a childhood bike wreck or something like that, but there would be time for that story later.

"Your hair is amazing." I let my fingers wander close

—but not too close—to her breast. Her eyes widened, and I saw her pulse pound in her throat. That's when I realized that, professional or not, I wanted her. I wanted to hold her, please her, and make her see all the stars I could give her…and money had nothing to do with it.

"What do you say we move over to a table, maybe order some dinner?"

She looked down at my hand on her hair and looked back up at me.

"I'm hungry. Let's do it."

Booyah.

CHAPTER 6

BELLE

A thought kept running through my head.
Holy shit.

I was out with an escort. In public.

Could people tell by looking at me? Or were they just wondering, "How'd that girl end up with that specimen of human perfection?"

Yeah, that's probably what they were thinking.

Cripes. I wasn't really even sure what a male escort was. Why hadn't I asked Jackie? Or even Zenia when I'd had the chance? She knew all my other dirt, she might was well know I had no idea what to do with the freaking gorgeous man she'd set me up with. Well, not exactly set me up with—I *was* paying, after all. Okay, I wasn't paying. Jackie was.

But still, I felt like a teenager who'd just gotten her

license and been handed the keys to a brand-new Ferrari. I had no idea what the hell to do with this man sitting next to me.

Was I supposed to chat him up, flirt with him, make him want me? Or was he supposed to be the seducer—try to get in my head, and maybe in my pants?

What was the protocol here?

And why hadn't I thought this through, before I was in that fancy restaurant, in a fancy hotel, in the fanciest of L.A. neighborhoods?

Shit.

"Have you been here before?" I managed to croak after we'd been seated in a private corner with menus.

He nodded, gazing directly at me. Maybe too directly, because his eyes were so piercing and his face so handsome I couldn't freaking think.

"I have," he said finally, totally honest. "A few times."

Of course he had. Places like that were made for people like him, with their mod-chic décor, dim lighting, and waitstaff who floated by as if they had no legs.

"What about you? Have you been here?" he asked, completely serious. Maybe it was his job, or maybe he was blind…but he kept complimenting me, treating me like I belonged in places like this. With the beautiful people.

I took a sip of wine to stifle a laugh—I'd spotted a plate of fifty-dollar pasta on the menu served with something called 'ramps.' Despite the common-sounding name, I knew they must have been some super-cool vegetable harvested by happy elves deep in a magical forest somewhere. Undoubtedly worth fifty dollars. Maybe even more.

Seriously, was he kidding? "No, I've not been here. I tend to go to places like House of Waffles."

Shit. Now why had I gone and said that? He was going to think I was the biggest hick. Then again, considering where I was from, it wasn't that far off.

He smiled. Oh great…not only did he now know I was a hick but also probably knew all about my likes and dislikes and found my ideas quaint and hilariously backward. "Oh my god. I love House of Waffles. That place is the *best*," he said.

Huh?

"Are you serious? You *like* that place?" I looked around the restaurant and was pretty sure Tom Cruise was seated in the far corner. Damn their fancy low light. "I mean, I thought, you know, that *this* was your kind of place."

"What? Are you kidding? I mean this place is great," he said as he gestured around the restaurant, "but nothing beats House of Waffles. For Christ's sake, I dream about their curly fries."

"Oh my god," I gushed happily. "Those fries are legendary."

"They sure as hell are," he said, nodding wistfully. He jiggled the ice in his scotch and drained his last sip.

And damn if those lips, wet with expensive scotch, didn't look delicious.

He beckoned one of the waitstaff floating by and leaned toward me over the table.

"Wanna go?" he asked.

"What? Where?"

Shit. Were we supposed to jump into sex so early in the evening? I mean, I thought we'd at least eat first.

"Finish your wine. Let's get out of here."

Oh my god.

"And go where?" I asked firmly.

He titled his head at me, like maybe I was nuts. "To the House of Waffles. Are you kidding? My mouth is watering for curly fries right now. And I won't say anything if you order a triple order covered with garlic. Because that's my jam."

"Serious?" I asked. This guy knew how to speak my language.

"Yeah. Let's do it." He threw some money on top of the bill the waiter had delivered.

I gulped my wine in one big sip as he stood. And as if the night hadn't already had enough surprises, he extended his hand.

To me. Like, to hold my hand. Xander, who was so gorgeous I could hardly breathe when looking at him, wanted to take my hand.

So I gave it to him.

His car was valet-parked because that's what everyone

in L.A. did, and when it arrived in front of us, delivered by a smiling little guy in a bow tie, I almost fainted. I mean, I worked at a freaking car dealership in freaking Beverly Hills, so I saw amazing cars all day long. But I'd never ridden in anything like what I was looking at just then.

Xander pulled open a long, shiny red passenger door, but I didn't move to get in. I was frozen, my feet stuck to the ground.

"What is this?" I asked, my gaze running from one long end of the car to the other. Seriously, I had no idea that cars like it still existed.

"It's a '67 Cadillac Coupe DeVille. I restored it myself."

"Wow," was all I could manage. I ran my hand over the spotless paint that had been waxed to perfection. There was a term the guys in the service shop used for a car in perfect condition... cherry. This car was cherry.

His hand slipped from the car door to my waist, and I was suddenly able to move my feet again. Just a few feet away, two valet guys were drooling over the car, nudging each other and speculating on its engine size.

"Belle, if you get in it, I can take you for a ride in it."

"Right." I jumped in and pulled a lap belt across my dress. And really quickly, before Xander could climb into the driver's side, I ran a finger across my teeth for a lipstick check. Clean.

The car floated into traffic, turning heads from every direction.

"This is amazing. How long have you had it?" I asked.

"Couple years," he admitted. "I picked it up at an estate sale, where it'd been sitting in a garage for two decades. It took me some time to restore her."

I stole a look at his flawless profile while he scanned left and right at a busy intersection. He slipped his hand over the buttery leather bench seat, which looked like it could have easily sat two more adults, and took my mine. Again.

Would it have been weird to ask him to just drive around all night? Maybe even forever? I was in the freaking coolest car in the universe, holding hands with the kind of man who made my pits sweat and my mouth run dry. And if I had to admit, another part of my body was getting warm and wet, too. Why spoil it with an ending? It was pure perfection.

But all too soon we pulled into House of Waffles. As disappointed as I was, my mouth was watering to share curly fries with Xander.

"Has L.A. been good to you, so far?" he asked after we settled into a booth, quickly placing our order, fries covered with the works.

Damn if he didn't stare right into my eyes as he spoke. And his gaze did not wander down to my cleavage at all. Well, except for when he reached for a curly fry, which he placed in my mouth. A little blob of ketchup fell, and feeling sexy for probably the first time in my life, I scooped it up with my finger and sucked it clean. For him.

I'd never been to House of Waffles at night, and I didn't recognize anyone working there, which was just as well. I didn't need anybody in my business.

"L.A. has worked out well for me, so far."

Oh, hell. What was I saying? L.A. had saved my freaking life.

"Actually, let me answer that again," I said.

He laughed. "Okay…"

"L.A.'s been great. I mean, I hardly have my dream life, but I'm getting there. I left a bad past behind, nothing to get into now but… yeah, it was pretty Lifetime Movie of the Week– level bad. But I've got some great friends, and am preparing for a career. So, it's coming together."

The waitress returned with two giant vanilla shakes. Xander peeled the wrapping off two straws, then raised his glass in toast.

"Here's to L.A.," he said. "The land of new beginnings."

When we were nearly comatose with fries and milkshakes, we waddled out to the red Caddy, each weighing more than we did when we went in. Xander opened my door, but before I could climb in, his hand caught my chin, and he tilted my face toward his. I knew what was coming, and thank goodness the car was there, because god knew I needed something to hold on to.

His lips slid over mine, softly at first, as if seeking permission. And as they did, the most surprising thing was how natural it was, as if the kiss were the logical next turn of events in an already perfect evening. When his lips parted, I tumbled into a bottomless pit of desire, my eyes fluttering closed while his warm mouth moved over mine.

"How would you feel about going to your place?" he asked.

Oh, my.

"My car's at the hotel."

"Let's go get it. I'll follow you home," he said.

I gave him a small smile and slipped back into the soft leather passenger seat. This time I was the one to reach for *his* hand.

As we got to my place, with his Caddy right behind me all the way across town, I did a full scan of the parking lot, just like I always did. It was a habit I just couldn't seem to break, and one I suppose I never would. Fear did that to you, as did a violent ex-husband.

But for the moment, at least, I was safe. And nervous as hell.

I'd just have him up for a cup of tea, maybe, and then send him on his way. I supposed you could do more with a male escort if you wanted, but I wasn't sure I wanted to, and besides, I didn't exactly have a boatload of experience in the sack. I had no doubt he'd see that right off the bat, and I didn't want him thinking I was pathetic or otherwise feeling sorry for me.

He waited for me as I climbed out of my VW. "So this is where you live?" he asked, looking at the cluster of apartments above an ugly little strip mall with a pizza place on one end and a laundromat on the other.

I nodded while fumbling with my key at the security door. "Yup."

Then he looked at me. I mean, yeah, he'd been looking at me all evening—he was polite that way. But that time he *looked* at me. He saw me. Maybe he saw *through* me, as they say. I couldn't be sure.

And that made me even more nervous than I already was.

Once inside the building, he followed me through the dingy lobby to my apartment.

"Can I get you some coffee? Tea?" I asked, after I'd kicked off my heels, wondering when he was going to ask, or maybe not ask but just realize, that his services had been gotten as a gift from a friend.

"Coffee sounds great, with sugar if you have it," he said, looking around. "Cute place."

"Yeah, it's small, but it's very safe and private—"

Shit. No need to start talking about that stuff.

But as I walked past him to get the coffee going, he put his hand on my arm, gently turning me toward him. He pushed the hair off my shoulders, and smoothed it down my back.

What was it about this guy? I'd never known a man who'd watched for my reaction to his touches. *He* wanted to accommodate *me*.

"Are you cold?" he asked, running his hands up and down my arms. I realized that from my bare arms all the way down to my wrists I was covered in goose bumps, and every hair on my arms stood up straight.

"No. More like nervous." I bit my lip.

"I get that. I do. And we won't do anything you don't want to. Okay?" He placed his hands on either side of my face and waited for my response.

"Thank you," I said, tension flowing out of me, replaced with the undercurrent of arousal that had been flooding me for over an hour now. "Thank you so much."

"You're welcome." He bent down and placed a kiss on my forehead. Then he took my hand and led me to the bedroom.

Guess we weren't having coffee.

He kicked off his shoes and lay down, pulling me with him. He ran his fingers through my hair again.

"You're beautiful. So beautiful," he whispered.

He rolled me onto my back, his hand smoothing

down my dress until he reached its hem. When his warm hand landed on my thigh, I shivered in repressed need, so long held back that until that instant I'd forgotten I even had it, and I pressed to kiss him harder. I couldn't help it.

"You okay, Belle?" he asked.

"Mmmm," was all I could manage.

His hand wandered under my dress, lifting it a bit more with each stroke of my thigh until he hooked a finger in the waistband of my panties. He tickled my stomach before lowering the delicate lace, stopping to look at me and check in. My knees parted, telling him all he needed to know.

In a second, my dress was up to my hips, panties on the floor. He was lowering himself, moving toward my—

Oh no. Not that.

"Um. Xander. That's okay. You don't have to, you know."

He paused and looked up at me.

"What do you mean I don't *have* to?" he asked, his face a question mark.

"Well. I know guys don't really like that, and you don't have to."

"Belle. If a man doesn't want to kiss your most private parts, well then he doesn't deserve you. It's not dirty. It's not nasty. It's beautiful. Besides, I happen to like it."

Um. I didn't know *what* to say to that. My fantasy,

and he actually wanted to do it? I was suddenly nervous again. What if I didn't taste good?

Xander could see my worries and smiled. "Relax, darling. If you don't like it, I'll stop. But I think you will."

And somehow, dammit, he was right. When his tongue slipped between my folds, it was as if there was nothing else in the world. Pleasure shot from the sensitive bundle of nerves between my legs to my belly, where it spread like a wildfire. Within moments, I was writhing, gasping for breath, and grabbing for his hair. Oh my, with one lick, he'd made me an addict for life.

"You like getting your pussy tasted," he murmured, slipping one finger inside me and zeroing in on my clit with his soft lips.

I arched to push myself more fully to him when an orgasm slammed into me like an out-of-control freight train, leaving me breathless and racked with spasms.

"God, Xander...oh my god..." Convulsions racked my body, and I pounded the bed with my fists until I was too weak to move anymore.

He lay next to me, arms tight around me. He smelled of my scent—my sex—and it was such a goddamn turn-on, it was all I could dream about after I dozed off.

CHAPTER 7

XANDER

"Hello, Xander," Zenia said as I adjusted the phone against my ear. In the microwave, I had my breakfast—two oatmeal packets to mix with protein powder before hitting the gym. Always watching what I ate.

"How's my favorite girl?" I asked, trying not to get distracted by the rotating bowl. For some reason, watching microwaves is fascinating to me. Even as a kid, my parents had to yell at me to get away from the door while the popcorn was popping.

Her sultry laugh washed over me from the other end of the cellular line, and there went all thoughts about the microwave. "I always know when you're going to ask for something, Xander, because you lay on the flattery."

No doubt she had my number. I wasn't an ass kisser, but every now and then, flattery was called for.

"Well, you're right, Zenia. I *am* asking for something. But you are still my favorite girl. Well, one of them, anyway."

"I knew it," she chuckled, an office chair squeaking in the background. "One of the *many*. Say, how'd things go with Belle?"

Belle. Why did her name cause a twitch in my shorts?

Oh, right. Because not only was she hot as hell, but so was the evening we'd had together...

"She's very special, Zenia. It was a great evening."

"Xander, you describe every date as special. I know you."

She was on to something. But this had not been like the others.

"No, Zenia. It was a very different date. We went to House of Waffles."

"You went w*here?*" Zenia asked, shocked. "I booked you a reservation in one of the top twenty-five restaurants in Beverly Hills, and you go to a House of Waffles?"

"Let me explain before you go all ballistic on me," I reply quickly, laughing. Zenia, for all her good points, was the antithesis of House of Waffles. "You taught me that I gotta trust my instincts, and I was right on this. She's a down-to-earth girl who loves curly fries and vanilla shakes."

Just like me, I might add. But I didn't.

"Good lord. If it got out that my escorts took their dates to dumps like that—"

"Stop," I interrupted. "Cut out the snobby bullshit."

There was absolute silence on the other end of the phone, and for an instant I was worried I'd taken it too far. Zenia wasn't used to being called out. But I knew I'd read the situation correctly and had shown Belle a good time.

And I'd had a hell of a time, too.

That was why I felt so bad about my dickish move.

After Belle had fallen asleep, I'd tucked her in, and split. It was an agency rule. No spending the night with clients.

She'd dozed off holding my hand, and when I was certain she was sound asleep, I slipped out of the bed and found a piece of paper to leave a note on. But before I took off, I watched her sleep for a couple of minutes, her long blond hair splayed across the bed. I felt like a goddamned stalker, but she was just so beautiful, her head propped on the pillow, her lips parted just enough to make a soft girl-snore.

Zenia sniffed. "What is your request, Xander? I do hope it's not…unreasonable."

"I have a second audition coming up for a movie that might be made with Arnie. Do you think you could reschedule some of my clients for me? I'll owe you."

A big sigh sounded from the other end of the line. I

knew she hated to reschedule clients. Hell, I hated it, too. You get all excited, and then poof, you're asked to choose another date. Kinda killed some of the magic.

"Xander, I'll do what I can and consult with you on the rest. But please don't make a habit of this. No one wants you to get your big break more than I do, but we have to keep our commitments. And quite honestly, there are a few clients who insist on just you."

Her little compliment, just slipped in there, was designed to make me feel special, but also like a heel for asking to move clients. "I'll make it up to you, Zenia. And I promise, I'll try to handle the clients that I can. Thank you."

Zenia chuckled. "Just get the part, okay? And thank me when you get that Oscar."

Not forty-five minutes later, I'd parked the Caddy and was hustling toward the movie studio's offices, dressed just as they wanted, in jeans and a fitted T-shirt. Apparently they wanted me to try out 'in role' this time. My agent had emailed me the lines I'd be reading, but the main reason they wanted to see me was to review my martial arts moves and see how I looked in street clothes.

Growing up a military brat, I took every kind of martial arts class my mother could find. She figured it was a way to bring some stability to the disruption of our frequent moves, and it helped an energetic kid like me find an outlet for himself. I suppose it was good thinking on her part, although when I was a kid I'd hated getting used to the students and instructors in one studio, only to have to try and find a place for myself in another one every time we moved. I mean, it was better than doing football or soccer, but still sucked having to re-prove myself every time.

But I ended up being pretty good, and that's what I hoped would help me get the acting break I needed.

I mean, escorting was great, even if I did get into it because there weren't many other options for supporting myself at the time. My first job, parking cars, had barely kept a roof over my head, even with tips. L.A. was an expensive town, and I was not satisfied with being broke. I had more ambition than that. A lot more.

"Name please?" a disinterested woman asked, after looking me up and down.

"Johnson, Xander."

She checked something off on her clipboard,

"Take a seat over there, Mr. Johnson," she said with a toss of her head and started walking away, high heels *clump-clumping* down the hallway.

All righty then…at least I had an appointment, which was way better than the cattle calls where you just showed up and took a number.

I had no idea why, but I was dying to tell Belle

about my audition. The girl knew what it was like to want something, and the hard work it took to get it.

And the way she'd moaned when I buried my face in her delicious pussy...

Shit. I had to stay off that kind of thinking, or I'd end up in my audition with an erection. But the sounds she'd made when I'd made her come...

"Mr. Johnson, we're ready for you now."

Heads turned my way as the other guys sized me up while I headed for the audition room. I couldn't blame them. Shit, I'd done the same thing to the guys who went before me.

In this business, when you were still a nobody, you were always checking out the competition.

Where they bigger?

Stronger?

Tougher?

Better looking?

I tried not to compare myself. Seriously. They say comparison is the thief of joy. But you could only stay magnanimous for so long in the dog-eat-dog world of acting. After a while, rejections would pile up on you, and it was easy to feel like you'd never make it, so why keep trying, etcetera, etcetera...

I didn't listen to those little voices. Fuck 'em.

I entered a plain room with several people clustered at a portable conference table. It was amazing how every audition room looked alike after a while. White walls, a folding meeting table, and people staring at you like you're a dog in the pound, is about the closest I could come to describing it in one sentence.

I made my way down the table, shaking everyone's hands.

"Mr. Johnson, my name's Ava Pierce, and I'm the director for this film." Ava clasped my hand just a bit longer than necessary. "After seeing your first tape, I just have to say it's so nice to meet you."

It was only when there was a bit of distance between other folks and me that I realized the director, the one who'd lingered with my hand, was pushing her tits together and licking her lips. Christ.

She saw buff guys all day long. Did she hit on all of them?

Her gaze particularly lingered on my crotch area, and part of me wondered if I should have chosen looser jeans to hide what Sandy called my 'bubble butt,' and other body parts.

"Mr. Johnson, you have the look we're searching for. Let's hear how you read your lines. Then we'll have you demonstrate your martial arts skills."

"Ready when you are," I said, quickly refocusing. It was times like that that I really could have bowed down to Zenia for all the lessons she'd taught me working for her. In just a few seconds, I was ready. And calm.

The horny director threw a line at me. Without missing a beat, I threw mine back at her.

We volleyed like that for five minutes, until one of the folks at the table raised his hand and said, "Stop."

Heads turned in his direction. He wasn't Arnie, who was nowhere in sight, but instead a slender, older man, possibly a producer or someone else on the team. He hadn't introduced himself beyond the name Steve when we shook.

"I want to see him with Melanie," Steve said.

There were murmurs of approval.

"Good idea."

"Let's do it."

"Somebody go get her."

First chance I could get, I asked, "Who is Melanie?"

The director, who was still staring at my crotch, almost giggled in hormonal glee. "Oh, Melanie. You may not know her now, but you will soon."

She looked up and down the table at her colleagues, who nodded in obedient agreement. When I obviously needed more clueing in, she explained further.

"Melanie is the next Gwyneth Paltrow. The world is going to love her."

The audition room door blew open, and a tall, skinny blonde with a slight overbite entered. She giggled and waved at everyone.

She was the next Gwyneth Paltrow? I mean, I got it, not every actress was beautiful, but unless she was a miracle worker once the cameras rolled, she was not the next Gwyneth Paltrow.

"Melanie, meet Xander Johnson. I thought I'd have you two read together."

Melanie extended her hand and giggled as an assistant handed us lines to read.

"Why don't you start, Melanie?" the director asked.

Clearing her throat, Melanie launched into her lines, and I responded to her. It wasn't easy reading something I'd not seen before, but I went with it. What was the worst that could happen?

I might not get the role.

Yup. And that happened nine and a half times out of ten already, anyway.

We were flying through our pages, when I noticed, a few lines down, I was to kiss the female lead. I didn't know if they chose these pages to throw me off, but I was ready for anything.

At the right moment, I buried a hand in Melanie's hair and pulled her toward me. My lips landed on hers, and for a moment, it was the previous night at House of Waffles and I was with Belle, tasting and exploring her beautiful mouth.

I must have gone on too long, because someone hollered, "*Cut!*"

I stepped away, and Melanie stood there with her mouth open and stars in her eyes. I casually wiped my lips with my thumb and forefinger. "Sorry, everybody. Guess I got a little carried away."

Either I'd done something very right or very wrong, because Melanie was blushing like a tomato, and the director's mouth hung open. I looked down the row of people at the table, and they were all smiling and nodding.

And actually, I was smiling, too. It was fucking awesome to pretend I was with Belle again, even if it were only for a moment.

Damn. I had to see her again.

But I couldn't. At least not unless she set up a date with me. A paid date, that was. Zenia had one absolute rule that could not be broken by any of her escorts…no seeing a client outside of paid work. Not without her permission, and she rarely if ever gave permission. Which meant I had to wait. And be patient. And I somehow knew that wasn't going to happen. I sensed there was some rule-breaking in my not-too-distant future.

"Mr. Johnson, great job today. We're going to consider you for a bigger role than the one you originally came in for."

Holy shit. That never happened. Normally I'd hear 'nice, but maybe you'd like a role as waiter number three,' instead.

But I played it cool and shook hands all the way down the table again. Until I got to the horny director, who for some reason only Hollywood could explain, rose from her chair, hooked her arm through mine, and walked me to the door.

There, she looked back over her shoulder and lowered her voice as she held something close to her chest. "Here's my card. It would be lovely to see you again."

I smoothly untangled myself from her and accepted the card. She might have thought she was a man-eater, but I could handle myself around just about anything.

While it had seemed like a great audition, and I'd had the pleasure of meeting 'the next Gwyneth Paltrow,' I knew better than to get my hopes up. I called my agent to fill her in and then tried to push it out of my mind.

Since I'd had my clients rescheduled, thanks to Zenia, I had the day free and found myself thinking about the lovely Belle. That long, silky hair, and the way she'd come when I went down on her. I wasn't sure, but the way she reacted, it seemed like her first time. The simple idea that I was able to initiate her into such pleasure was sexy as hell.

And now I was getting a hard-on while driving down Sunset Boulevard.

I found myself headed toward The Agency. I needed to talk to Zenia.

"Hey, beautiful," I said, giving her a peck on the cheek as she opened the door. Being able to just walk in without her being busy was a rare treat.

"How was the audition?" she said, looking stunning as always, today in a sky-blue ensemble that accented her legs. "Tell me everything."

I followed her to her office, taking the time to organize my thoughts.

"I think it went well. You know how it is—it's hard to tell. You never know."

She nodded. "I remember those days."

I fidgeted in my seat, wondering suddenly why I was there. It felt like there was a blockage in my head, and Zenia saw it perfectly.

"Looks like you came here for a reason," she said. "Just talk, Xan. I've got time, and you're worth it."

That was Zenia, always knowing how to help me relax. "Well, I wanted to thank you for covering for me today so I could go on the audition."

She smiled. I knew she wanted me to succeed. It was part of the reason I'd do anything for her. We had each other's backs.

"Is that all?" she asked, raising a finely sculpted eyebrow.

I nearly spilled that I'd hoped to see Belle again but thought better of it. She'd tell me to steer clear, and if I went against her wishes—well, that would not be good.

So, I rose from my chair. "Yeah, I guess. I just wanted to say that I'll still try to handle what I can, and I'm heading down to work out."

She titled her head. "That's all?" she asked.

"Yup. Thank you again."

She looked at me with her Mona Lisa smile and said nothing.

Damn, she knew me well. Possibly too well.

CHAPTER 8

BELLE

My eyes wouldn't focus. Not on anything. Not on the computer in front of me, not on the blinking phone screaming for me to answer it—not even on people who came by my desk. Nothing.

It's not that I was tired. No, that was not the problem. The truth was, I'd slept better than I had in—well, I don't know how long. Certainly since I'd been in L.A. The way Xander had made me feel, like I was freaking queen of the world—yes, me, a sexy, desirable woman —had lulled me into a sound and peaceful sleep. The only thing that made it better were his arms around me.

Until they weren't.

And that's what killed it. I woke up, stretched,

rolled over...and Xander was freaking *gone.* Without even a trace of his aftershave left behind.

Yup. I woke up just about the happiest I'd ever been, and boom, I was all alone. Just like I'd been for every night since I gotten to L.A. Just like, it felt like as I stared at my clock and wondered if I'd dreamed it all, I could be for the rest of my life. The thought nearly brought tears to my eyes, and I blinked them back. No...it wasn't going to be that way.

Getting out of bed, I saw there was a note. I had to hand him that.

Beautiful Belle—I had great evening.
I have to head home now,
but hope to see you again sometime soon.
Your Xander

Gee. Thanks. Well, I guess that was better than a text message with kissy emojis.

I was an idiot for expecting anything more. It hadn't been a date—not a real date, anyway. I'd *paid* him to hang out with me, I knew that. But I'd been so comfortable with him, and what was even more telling was how comfortable he'd been with *me.* We went to the goddamn House of Waffles, for heaven's sake. You can't tell me the average girl who hires an escort would be happy going to the House of Waffles.

And yet I woke up alone. I guess I had no right to be

bent out of shape. He'd fulfilled his end of the bargain. Transaction, if you would.

Shit that word made me cringe. Reducing a night of fun and fantasy to a credit card statement on par with ordering Chinese delivery. Expensive Chinese delivery. But that's what it was.

And if that was the case, why was I so distracted that I couldn't see two feet in front of me? What the hell was that all about, and what was I going to do about it? God, I was an idiot. I never should have listened to Jackie, and I never should have gone to The Agency.

Taking a break to clear my head, I grabbed a cup of shitty coffee from the waiting room, downed it in three spasmodic gulps in order to skip the burned motor oil taste, and returned to reception to find Jackie waiting for me.

"Heya," she said, looking me up and down.

I wanted to tell her you couldn't tell if someone had just had sex just by looking at them, but I didn't want to get into it. She'd insist that yes, she most certainly could tell.

"Hi," I said with a deep sigh. "What's up?"

"What the hell happened to you? Either it went really bad, or really good." She looked at me with raised eyebrows, but I just shrugged. I wasn't going to be cracked that easily.

"C'mon. Spill it," she said impatiently after a few moments.

"I don't know, Jackie. I don't really feel like talking about it."

"Christ, girl. I need to know, did everything go okay? Are you all right?" She looked ready to deck someone. "I swear, if I have to, I'll march down there and—"

"Yes, yes, I'm fine," I reassured her before she could cause a scene. I didn't think Zenia would have appreciated a pissed-off car saleswoman kicking in her front door. "Calm down," I told her.

"So. It was good? I know that look…" she said, grinning. "And that wobbly walk across the floor this morning."

I nodded and sighed. Oh, what the hell. "Yeah. It was good. Amazing even."

"And, now you're in love with the guy."

"I am not!" I protested, keeping my voice low. "It was one night! I'll never see him again."

She really was ridiculous.

"Are you sure?" she asked.

"Are you crazy? I don't even know the guy."

"You know, he's one of the only men at The Agency I've never been with," Jackie mused.

Christ, how many escorts had she hired over the years?

She must have read my thoughts, and continued. "You know, every now and then I just want to spend time with someone good-looking and nice, who's actually gonna listen to me talk for a while rather than flap his gums all about himself. Of course, the sex is the icing on the cake." She gave me a deep, exaggerated wink, and part of me wondered if she had a points card for The Agency in her purse. Hire nine guys, get the tenth for free. The service shop at the dealership did the same for oil changes.

"Well, I didn't have sex with him," I said.

"*What?*" she nearly shrieked. "Are you kidding me? You had him in the palm of your hand and you didn't… seal the deal?"

"I didn't. I mean we did some stuff. But not, you know, all the way."

She looked like she was suppressing a laugh. Screw her.

"Sweetie," she started, "we're not twelve years old, and this ain't back home where the female orgasm is a mysterious scandal. You don't have to call sex *going all the way.*"

"All right. What do you think I *should* call it?" I was getting tired of the conversation and wishing the damn phone would ring and save me.

"Well, most people call it sex. But personally, I prefer the term *fucking*. Nothing better than a deep, long, hard-pounding fucking. In my opinion, anyway."

The boss was making his way toward us.

I reached for the phone to pretend to answer it. "Don't look now, but Ted's on his way. We'll have to wait to discuss *fucking* till lunch."

Jackie jerked her head around, and smiled brightly at Ted, as if she'd been expecting him.

"I'll pick you up at lunchtime. We can go to House of Waffles."

I didn't have the heart to tell her I'd just been there. Or did she already know?

Through the rest of the morning, I couldn't stop thinking about him. There I was, leaning against the brick wall of the car dealership, waiting for Jackie to finish with her customer, who was haggling over every last cent, so we could go to lunch. And all I could think about was the night before.

And, of course, the beautiful Xander.

The way he'd run his tongue up and down my slick folds...I'd never even thought my body could feel so good.

"Hey, ready?" Jackie asked, flashing me a thumbs-up and heading for her car so fast I had to trot to keep up. "Guess what? Another sale! Booyah, someone slap your mama!"

We got to our usual booth for lunch, something we nearly always managed as long as we got there by eleven forty-five.

Jackie ordered her usual, but I opted for the curly fries. It didn't matter that I'd had them just the night before. Ordering them again was an extension of the perfect evening, something I was desperate to hang on to.

"So, what'd you think of him?" Jackie asked. "Tell me he wasn't sex on a stick."

"Extremely handsome and hot." I stuffed my mouth with fries.

But that was not enough for Jackie. "C'mon. Tell me more."

I leaned toward her and lowered my voice. "He went down on me. It was my first time. Ever."

Jackie stopped, a huge chunk of lettuce on fork a halfway to her mouth. "No. That cannot be true. Please tell me that you did not just drop into Los Angeles from bum-fuck West Virginia, where you'd never, ever had your carpet munched?"

I nodded and sighed. "Yup. The ex-hubs never wanted anything to do with it. Said it was dirty and gross."

She rolled her eyes. "Good riddance to that fucker. God knows what he'd say if you'd asked for a tossed salad. Which, by the way, you should try. So...did ya like it?"

I had a feeling the 'tossed salad' she was referring to was nothing like what she had before her, but something that happened between consenting adults. Anyway, because she was the one who'd sent me to The Agency, maybe I owed her some naughty talk?

"It doesn't matter." I shrugged, still unwilling to say that the moment I came, it felt like time had stopped, the ground shook, and every problem I'd ever had disappeared into the atmosphere. "I'll never see him again, anyway."

She just kept staring at me, breaking me down with the same doe eyes and silent treatment she used whenever a customer was being a pain in the butt with her. And just like a customer, she wore me down.

"Yes, okay. I did like it. It was awesome and I can't stop thinking about it. I fell asleep in his arms. But he was gone when I woke up."

"Ya have a little crush on him, then," she said, unsurprised about the last part. Maybe it was normal in the escort biz?

"I don't know about that…"

Oh, who the hell was I fooling?

"Maybe. A little." Shit. My face was on fire. Blushing again. Dammit.

Jackie said nothing, just grinned a little, so I continued. "I mean, c'mon. How can you talk to someone for hours, really connect, and then get all intimate and not feel anything? I'm just not like that." I looked out the window into the parking lot.

Jackie reached for my hand. "I know what you mean, sweetie. Why can't they all be like that? Speaking of which, do you think I should try him?"

Huh? Was she fucking kidding?

Oh. Wait. It wasn't like he was my boyfriend or anything. She could do whatever the hell she wanted. Just like *he* could.

Determined to get my big O of the night before off my mind, I shot over to a nearby yoga studio after work to get my head on straight. But I didn't go without trepidation. I hadn't been to yoga in ages, and I'd be lucky to reach my knees, never mind my toes.

The instructor, a waifish guy who could contort himself into a human pretzel, really was feeling his oats that day and cycled the group through a sequence of about twenty sun salutations like he was in a race against time. Of course, I was half a pose behind the class almost the entire time because all I could think about was how Xander, when he was between my legs making me feel like I'd died and gone to heaven, kept looking up at me as if to check in and make sure I was okay. Was that what a real lover was like? If so, I'd wasted far too much time with that shitty ex-husband. But I'd known that for a while.

If there was any benefit to my distracted mind, it was that I didn't feel the pain of the sun salutations in my hamstrings or arms even though everyone else was groaning. After practice, I pulled a sweatshirt over my head and walked out to my car. Just a few steps away from pressing *unlock*, I froze. The voices of the other students got more and more faint as they said their good nights to each other, climbed in their cars, and headed home. If I didn't move fast, I'd be all alone in the dark parking lot. But it was as if my feet had sunk into the asphalt and that if I tried too hard to move I'd break into a thousand pieces.

The car next to mine was the exact year, make, and model as my ex's. But in my panic, I'd not initially noticed it had Arizona plates, and not the West Virginia ones his car would have had.

Still. It was uncanny, as well as telling that something as simple as a familiar car could throw me for such a loop.

Just then, a hand landed on my shoulder. I shrieked.

"Belle? Are you all right?" It was the yoga instructor.

I was shaking too hard to give a proper answer, so I just nodded like an idiot.

"What's going on, honey?"

"I…I…"

Breathe, girl. Just breathe.

"I thought I saw something that reminded me of—"

Christ, I couldn't even say it. Not only was I petrified, I was also ashamed.

But I didn't have to say anything else.

"C'mon. Let's get you into your car. Are you okay to drive?" he asked.

He gently pulled me from my frozen spot toward my car, where I finally pressed *unlock,* and pulled open my car door.

"Thank you," I said.

"Are you okay to get home by yourself? You look awfully shaken."

"I'll be okay now. Thank you so much." I pulled the

car door closed and turned over the ignition. The instructor walked to his car, looking over his shoulder several times to see if I were actually capable of driving.

I took a deep breath as I backed out of my parking spot, alternatively relieved that the car next to mine belonged to a total stranger, and mad at myself for nearly having had a panic attack at seeing a car that looked like Todd's.

God, I hated that man.

But at least I wasn't thinking about Xander anymore.

CHAPTER 9

XANDER

Who the hell was calling me at six a.m.?

I reached for the phone on my nightstand, disrupting my cat's slumber and nearly knocking her to the floor. Yeah, so I had a cat. Big deal. Some people have dogs. Richard had an iguana of all things... I had a cat. That didn't make me weird, or feminine, or whatever. It certainly didn't make me the crazy cat lady of my neighborhood.

As Hamburger meowed his displeasure at me, I grabbed my phone.

Shit. It was my agent calling.

Most likely with bad news.

"Hey." I tried to disguise my sleepy voice. I was an actor after all. Well, trying to be an actor.

"Oh, Xander, I woke you up. I'm so sorry. Let me call you back later—"

"No," I interrupted. "I'm awake now. What's going on?"

Yeah, like I'd ever blow off a call from my agent.

"Well, I wanted to tell you they really liked your audition the other day," she said.

Okay...

"And apparently your chemistry with the next Gwyneth Paltrow starlet was off the charts."

I knew who I could thank for that.

I popped up in bed. "Yeah? So what's up? What else did they say?"

"You didn't get the main hero role," she said.

Fuck. Had someone just punched me in the gut? Because it sure felt like it.

Something in her voice stopped me from groaning in total depression.

"But you did get the other one. The hero's buddy. Which is still awesome."

No way. Holy shit.

I jumped out of bed. "Are you serious? *Fucking A!*" I shouted.

"I know, honey. I'm so proud of you. The read-throughs start in two weeks."

She blathered on about various details, but all I could think was *What? Two weeks?* I needed to rearrange my life and I had only two weeks?

But hey, it was what I'd wanted for as long as I could remember.

"One more thing, Xander."

"Yeah?" I asked, wondering how much I'd missed of what she'd been talking about.

"Don't shave. They're going to want you with a beard."

I wondered if Belle liked beards…

Maybe I was turning into a pussy, but all I could freaking think about was her. I wanted to call and tell her my good news. She'd appreciate it. She'd understand—she was that kind of woman.

She and I shared something. I learned that right off the bat. We were both the kind of people who set goals and went after them. Of course, not without a few bumps in the road along the way. Ambition was never a smooth line.

But I couldn't see her. I couldn't call her. And it was time I got used to that.

I made myself some breakfast and headed across town to The Agency.

"Xander!" Sandy called from across the street after I'd parked. He ran toward me, his distinctive double vent St. Laurent suit jacket flapping behind, while I waited for him to catch up.

"Hey," he said, clapping me on the back. "Bitch, I

just had a threesome with two awesome clients, both hung like horses—"

"Sandy, I don't talk about my dates, and you probably shouldn't talk about yours."

He rolled his eyes. "Fine, mister boy scout. You don't talk about your dates because you have crushes on all of them. Mine are all about boning, and nothing else—"

"Okay, San."

I pressed the buzzer at the front door to The Agency.

While we waited, Sandy looked me up and down. "How come so casual, amigo? I mean, not that you don't look good. You look awesome, actually. Very motorhead chic. You know, all butch and stuff."

I glanced down at my jeans and faded rock concert T-shirt. Shit. Maybe I should have dressed a little nicer, but I was just too excited.

"Nah, no clients. Just gotta talk to Zenia."

The moment I said her name, the door flew open and there she stood, stunning as always in some sort of silky yellow number that was the perfect contrast to her dark skin.

"Gentlemen." She stepped aside to let us in. "Come on in. I see you dressed for the occasion, Xander."

Sandy threw his arms in the air with his usual drama. "I know, right? So sloppy and yet somehow still so hot." He put his hands on his hips and nodded approvingly. "Seriously, sorta looks like an updated

George Michael…or maybe Springsteen since George played for my team."

"To what do I owe the pleasure of this visit, my friends?" Zenia asked, looking amused, as always, by Sandy's babbling.

"I wanted to have a chat with you," I said. "If you have a moment."

Sandy looked from one of us to the other, and when he realized I was referring to a conversation that didn't include him, rolled his eyes.

"Whatevs. I'm heading down to the gym to do some stretches and tone this fat ass. If anyone needs me," he called back over his shoulder. As he walked, he sang to himself. "Yeah…they love this fat ass, ha-ha!"

Zenia smiled and shook her head. "I'm glad there's soundproofing when Sandy's around. C'mon. Let's go up to my office. I didn't think I'd see you here again so soon. I hope you have good news."

When we were settled, she offered me tea, like she always did, and I accepted a steaming cup.

"What's going on, sweetie?"

I sank back into her must-have-cost-a-fortune suede sofa and looked around. I'd really miss the place.

"I got a call from my agent."

Her eyebrows rose. "Tell me."

"I got a role in the Schwarzenegger movie. Not the big role I'd hoped for, but something really good. Hero's best friend… I'll be in the opening credits."

Zenia jumped up to give me a kiss on the cheek.

"Oh Xander, I'm so happy for you. I know how hard you've worked for this…"

Never thought I'd see the day when Zenia actually teared up. But she sure as hell did, and I felt like a million bucks.

"I couldn't have done it without you," I replied gratefully, wishing I could say just how much without sounding like a total pussy. "You and your connections really helped me turn the corner. You know a hell of a lot of people, Zenia."

"I may have helped you get a good agent, but you got this movie with your talent."

"Thank you." Shit, now I was embarrassed.

"Are you still interested in taking on clients?" she asked, tapping her fingernail on her desk.

I'd known this question was coming. "That's what I had to talk to you about…I start in two weeks."

"Oh, okay. Well, you have plenty of time to see a few more clients, Xander."

It was tempting. I mean the money was good, and I was all about building on my nest egg to avoid living paycheck-to-paycheck like my family had. But Belle's face flashed through my mind, and something felt…off.

"I'm not able to do that, Zenia."

She tilted her head and stared me down. "I'm surprised to hear that."

I nodded.

"Is something going on, Xander?"

"I have some things to do, some things to get in

order, in the next two weeks. It's going to be hectic. I can do one last client—that party gig, but that's it."

"If that's the best you can do, then all right."

She had a look on her face, one I'd not seen before.

"You know, Xander, if you're leaving The Agency, it might be fun to get to know each other better. You know, socially, instead of professionally."

Her smile was sexy as hell. But, no. Booty calls were not my jam. Funny thing for an escort to say, but it was true.

"I'm flattered, Zenia. But that's not the sort of relationship I want with you. You're like a big sister."

A smile spread across her face, and she threw her head back with a laugh. "Well now, I think that's the first time I've ever been sister-zoned by one of my guys, but I think I like it. So, I will gladly continue to be your big sister. And cheer you on, every step of the way."

"Thank you, Zenia."

On my way out, I ran into Sandy again.

"Not working out?" I asked him on the way to the car.

"Eh. Changed my mind," he said, shrugging. "I just got a client, so I'll do my booty bridges tomorrow."

I nodded and couldn't hide my grin. Sandy was just too inquisitive for his own good. "Dude, I got a part in a movie."

Sandy's mouth dropped open, and then he shrieked,

attracting the attention of everyone up and down the street. "Oh. My. God."

He threw his arms around me. And didn't let go. I had to unwrap him from my neck, mostly because his relatively skinny arms were starting to cut off the blood to my brain. Seriously, that little guy had wiry strength. He could probably choke out a guy twice his size. "Congrats, Xander. I'm so happy for you. Hey, do you think you could get me a part? Like, I could be your fabulously fashionable gay bestie or something?"

"Let me get back to you on that, Sandy."

I knew where I was going before I even got behind the wheel of my car. Sometimes there were things you just had to do, and there was no doubt doing them was the right thing. And since I'd kinda given my notice to Zenia anyway…it wasn't really against the rules.

Twenty minutes of L.A. traffic later, I pulled into Beverly Hills Motors. I might end up regretting it, but it was a chance I had to take.

The second I was inside, a short woman with giant breasts stopped me with a finger in my face.

"I know you, don't I? Did you buy a car from me last year? You're back already for another? Well, I have some new models to show you."

She got a grip on my arm and leaned closer, lowering her voice and pressing her impressive fakies against my arm. A pretty good sales move...for most guys. "Since it's nearly the end of the month, I can make you a good deal. Just tell me what you want to spend and I'll get you in the car of your dreams."

I freed myself from her grip gently but surely. I wasn't there to waste time. "I'm not sure we've met before. I didn't buy a car from you last year. Or anybody else."

She snapped her head back and frowned. "I could have sworn I knew you from somewhere. What's your name?"

"Xander. Xander Johnson."

She looked me up and down, then brought her palm to her forehead and smacked herself. "I know you now. You're with," she lowered her voice to a whisper, "The Agency, aren't you?"

"I am."

But I'd never been on a date with her. I would have remembered.

She continued. "Oh, wait. I know your...*coworker*... Richard. In fact, I know him very well, if you know what I mean. I'm Jackie." She extended her hand and winked dramatically.

"Oh, you know Richard. Great guy. I'll tell him I saw you. Hey, can you tell me where Belle sits—"

"So *that's* why you're here. You're *that* Xander," she said, way too loudly.

Discretion, lady! Discretion! I wasn't worried about myself, but I did want Belle's privacy protected.

I finally spotted her and started moving in her direction.

But Jackie grabbed me first. "Hey, before you run off, I was thinking maybe we should get together sometime."

I wasn't about to burst her bubble with my life plans, but I wanted to be clear on things.

"I'm currently...booked up. But you know how to get in touch with Zenia, right?"

Her face lit up, like I'd just given her the best advice of her life.

"Yeah. I think I'll call her tonight." She looked out into the car lot. "But before you go, did you want to see some cars? Maybe take a test drive or two?"

Her grin was about as wide as Santa Monica Boulevard, and her words clearly said I could take more than a new car for a test drive if I wanted.

"No, Jackie. Maybe another time. If I were looking for new wheels, believe me, you're the first one I'd call."

She extended her hand.

"Thank you, Xander. Now, if you'll excuse me, I think I see a new customer out on the lot." And in a dust cloud of perfume and high heels, she was gone.

Whew. Next time, if there was a next time, I'd be prepared for her.

I approached the sprawling counter where Belle was juggling phones, customers, and looking back and forth between two huge computer monitors. I watched her for a minute like I had the first night we'd met and was struck all over again by her confidence as she dealt with the chaos around her.

She had no idea how great she was.

But I was about to show her.

She looked up, eyes scanning the showroom as she looked for someone. She tucked a long strand of blonde hair behind her ear and glanced my way.

CHAPTER 10

BELLE

X ander.

Oh my sweet lord, Xander was in the showroom.

Xander, who'd kissed and feasted on me until I nearly passed out and given me an orgasm I hadn't been able to stop thinking about.

What was he doing there, and why had I worn my absolute ugliest dress that day?

Dammit.

As if the day hadn't already been crazy enough. Things at the dealership always heated up at the end of the month—salespeople were frantic to meet their goals, and shoppers knew it was the best time to get a good deal. Add in the mid-production year factory sales, and you got...the perfect storm.

We might have been in ritzy Beverly Hills, but everyone wanted a bargain, no matter how loaded they were.

But Xander. He had a car—that gorgeous Caddy. Why the hell was he car shopping?

Oh. Wait. Maybe he wasn't car shopping.

One look at his face should have told me that. He was there to see me.

Shit, shit, shit.

And damn if he didn't look awesome in a pair of jeans hanging low around his hips and a faded old T-shirt, which, if my eyes weren't fooling me, had a teeny little hole right near the underarm.

A really cute, teeny little hole.

And his eyes. Goddamn those eyes.

As the phone rang off the hook, I pressed buttons and spoke into my headset without taking my eyes off him.

Because I was looking at the only thing I wanted to see at that moment.

"Miss? Miss? Are you okay?" asked a customer who was standing in front of me like he was King of California, tapping his Black American Express card on the counter. Confused, he looked back and forth between Xander and me, and then a smile crossed his face, as if he were witnessing a rare mating ritual.

Which I guess he had.

"I'm sorry, sir. I just saw a friend…I hadn't seen…in a long time."

I got to work with the customer, who was buying a brand-new car for his company. Out of the corner of my eye, I watched Xander leaning on the far end of the counter, far enough away to let me do my job, but close enough to make my hands shake.

Of course that would be that moment Ted joined the fracas.

"Sir, what may I help you with?" he said, extending his hand to Xander.

It was all I could do, not to laugh out loud.

"Oh, I'm waiting to see Belle, here," Xander said, gesturing in my direction. "I have some important business."

"Well, she doesn't sell cars, sir. But I have several other capable folks who could help you," Ted said, totally oblivious. He craned his neck across the showroom, waving Starla over.

Oh shit. Starla, the man-eater.

But Jackie came rushing past her and put her arm on Xander.

"I've got it, Ted."

"Oh. Great. Thank you, Jackie." He headed back to his corner, while Jackie looked at Xander like he was a bowl of cream and she was a starving kitten.

"Now Xander, I was thinking..." Jackie said, steering him away from the counter and *me*, toward a bunch of convertibles.

What. The. Fuck?

Had she been out with him? It sure looked like it, as

chummy as she was being with him. Damn. Okay. He nodded politely at whatever she was saying, occasionally glancing back over his shoulder at me, while she kept a firm grip on his forearm.

The one I'd run my fingers up and down just a couple nights ago.

Was I a chump or what?

"Beverly Hills Motors, how may I direct your call?"

I had to force my voice to remain steady. It wouldn't do to cry at work. What had I been thinking, anyway? That he'd come to see me? Like I was so damn special.

I was so done with men. Sad thing was, I'd never really even gotten started.

"He's hot, isn't he?" Starla asked, leaning over the counter toward me.

I couldn't speak.

"C'mon, sweetie. I saw you looking at him."

Would I get fired if I killed her? Because I wanted to really, really badly. And painfully. Could I shove my red Swingline stapler up her nose?

"Starla, I have a lot to do here." I faux tapped on the computer. Maybe that would get rid of her.

She sniffed. "Didn't take Jackie long to sink her hooks into that perfect specimen of manhood, did it?"

She looked to me for affirmation, but I kept my eyes locked on the computer.

That didn't stop her.

"I mean, Jackie's a pretty lady and all, but since she

got those new tits, she's all over every man who comes in here. Confidence up one side and right back down the other." She clicked her tongue as she shook her platinum curls. "Or maybe desperation. Needing a little reassurance."

Please go away. Please, please, please. I can't stand any more of your hypocritical bullshit at this moment in my life.

But she didn't go away. She just kept going. "Who is he, anyway? He's fucking gorgeous. Maybe when she's done with him, I can—"

"*Starla*. I have work to do. And I don't want to talk about that guy."

"Geez, honey. Would you relax? Okay. Do your thing." She waved her hand dismissively, and wandered off, but not without first fluffing her hair and ensuring her blouse fell open at just the right spot to show off her own wares.

I took several deep breaths and considered different ways to get through what was turning out to be one messed-up day.

"Belle. Got someone here to see you."

I looked up from my furious typing to find Jackie and Xander right in front of me, with Xander's gaze drilling into me with an intensity that left me holding the counter for balance.

Down, girl.

"I tried to sell him a car, " Jackie said, nudging him playfully and giving me a grin that told me she'd just pulled off an acting job that had even me fooled. "I really did. But he wouldn't bite, and when I saw that beauty he was driving, I understood why. I'll let you kids chat, and I'll go find my next victim."

She laughed and wandered off, but not before throwing a discreet wink my way. I wasn't sure if I wanted to smack her, hug her, or both. Probably both.

"Hey," Xander said quietly. "Sorry to interrupt your work."

"What are you doing here?" I looked around. So far, our conversation was private.

"I wanted to see you, obviously. I figured if it got awkward I could always pretend to be buying a car. I didn't know the salespeople would be on me like flies on shit."

"Well. That's how things work at a car dealership. But it's nice to see you."

He gave me a small smile that showed off the cleft in his chin. Damn him.

"It's very nice to see you," he said. "I didn't know how to reach you, but fortunately you'd told me where you worked."

"Looks like you and Jackie hit it off."

"What?" he said, glancing over his shoulder. "I told her I was here to see you."

"Oh." I wasn't sure how to react to that, except to remind myself that Jackie deserved a hug for saving Xander from Starla's clutches.

Xander looked back and me and smiled again, a megawatt smile that could have lit up downtown. "I wanted to invite you to dinner. Maybe someplace other than House of Waffles, this time?"

It was hard not to have my chin hit the desk. Wait, wha? I mean, was he really here, asking *me* out?

He leaned toward me. "But not a date like we had the other night. A real date. This weekend."

"Are you allowed to do that?" I asked. I was sure there had to be rules, and I didn't want anyone in trouble.

"No," he said "Not as an employee of The Agency. But I told Zenia I was resigning."

My stomach did a double backflip. Really hard and really fast.

"What? Why?"

"I got a role in a movie. You remember that one I told you about?" His smile was huge, and I nodded as an excited grin broke out on my face.

"No way. Oh my gosh, congratulations. That's awesome. I'm so happy for you." I wanted to jump up and down, but that would make Ted most unhappy.

"Thank you. I'm pretty happy about it, myself. Actually, I'm fucking thrilled," he said, laughing. He reached for my hand, weaving his fingers in mine. A warmth washed over me. "So, will you have dinner with me? In real-date land, not fake-date land?"

Like I would ever be able to say no to him. How could any woman?

"I'm free...all weekend." Actually, I was free every weekend.

My heart was pounding so hard I was afraid he might hear it. I scribbled my number on a piece of paper and pushed it toward him, not entirely convinced I'd actually hear from him. Maybe he did this with all his clients. I mean, I didn't know this man from Adam. In spite of how nice he seemed, he could be a total slimeball.

"You know, I don't do this with my clients. In fact, I've never done this at all. In case you were wondering."

On top of everything else, he was apparently a mind reader. He leaned on the countertop, watching me with that amazingly handsome face, his boy-next-door perfect looks hypnotizing me, and I just looked back, wondering if I were insane or not, but not really caring either way.

Jackie was the one to break us out of our little lovey-dovey haze. "Hey, kids. Ted's wondering why someone's not sold Studboy a car yet. So if you're just loitering to flirt with our pretty girl here, you'd better not stick around for much longer."

Xander grinned, giving Jackie a nod but reaching for me with one hand. "Well, I guess I'm busted, then. I'll take off."

He gave my hand a nice squeeze before he released it.

"I'll see you ladies later. Don't work too hard."

I couldn't take my eyes off him and his cute behind as he walked out the door. Neither could Jackie, Starla, or any of the other females in the showroom. And as he left, I swear I heard a dozen simultaneous admiring sighs.

∼

My mood was soaring—a feeling I'd not had since, well, I couldn't actually remember the last time. An amazing guy—nice *and* gorgeous—wanted to hang out with me. When did that ever happen?

It was long past my break time, and if I wanted to be ready for the evening's accounting class, I needed to clock out for a bit and do some quick studying. I grabbed my backpack, intent on finding quiet corner to do some cramming. But how in the hell was I going to concentrate, now? All I could see were Xander's cool blue eyes, not to mention the hot way those slightly baggy blue jeans hung on his hips.

I skipped up the steps to the break room.

Xander Johnson wanted a date with *me*!

I opened my book on a sticky lunch table and worked my way over the lesson I'd reviewed the night before on payroll deductions. My accounting instructor loved nothing more than to call on random people with questions and test us on the fly. Scary as hell, but it ensured you were ready for class.

As I skimmed my notes, my phone vibrated. Without looking away from my book, I felt through my backpack's pockets till I found the little bugger.

I swiped *open* to find I'd missed a couple emails, as

well as a dozen or so phone calls. And they were all from an unknown number.

Huh.

Only a handful of people had this phone number. Literally. Like fewer than five.

My euphoria over Xander fizzled, slowly replaced by a sense of dread that had, over time, become a sort of sixth sense, not to mention a regular feature in my life.

I scrolled through my phone's *recent* list and found there'd been numerous missed calls every day of the past week. And just as I was looking, the phone rang again. I swiped it open, but no one was there.

Maybe it was nothing. Just those annoying robo solicitation calls, which kept dialing your phone until you either answered the call or blocked the number.

No need to freak out. Right?

I mean, they couldn't have been from my ex. For one, there was no way he could have gotten my number. And for another, he was off in the Caribbean.

That's what Nina had told me, and she knew what was going on in our small West Virginia town.

I turned back to my textbook, but it was too late. No studying was going to happen.

CHAPTER 11

XANDER

I t was exquisite torture, waiting three days to see Belle again. My hands itched to call her, to go over to her place and have a taste of her. It all actually twisted my stomach.

God I was turning into a pussy.

But with each morning, I woke with incredible anticipation, and when she finally had a day off, we piled into the Caddy and headed to Topanga Canyon for a hike.

The wait was worth it. The day was beautiful. It was one of those that seem to only be possible in California, where blue skies lifted you and the sunlight baked your skin until you were warm but never hot. And of course, the ocean—the deep, dark blue ocean stretching forever.

And Christ, did Belle look adorable in her hiking boots, her hair pulled into a long braid that hung forward over her shoulder.

As we approached our destination, I reached across the bench seat for her hand.

"Does Zenia know we're hanging out?" she asked, entwining her fingers with mine.

"Not exactly…" I admitted, shrugging.

"What do you mean, 'not exactly'? Either she does, or she doesn't." She laughed. "Please don't say you're creepin' on your job."

"Okay. Since you asked, we're not allowed to see clients outside of work arrangements."

She turned from her view of the ocean, toward me. "So is this a work arrangement?"

God, she was a ball buster. I loved it.

"No, it is not. And I think you know that. But, I'm resigning, anyway, so it's all good.

The wind from her open window whipped stray hairs around her face. So goddamn beautiful.

"But even if I weren't," I said, "it would be worth it."

"I'll take that as a compliment," she said, flashing that crooked smile at me.

At the top of the hill, I parked the Caddy in a pullout at the entrance to my favorite hike.

Belle popped out of the car and stood overlooking the broad canyon before us, to the Pacific Ocean far below.

"It's amazing. So beautiful," she said softly.

I draped an arm around her shoulder, although I was dying to touch her more intimately. But that could wait. I was a patient man.

"Personally, I love Los Angeles," I said, scanning the horizon for container ships headed for port. "Some people hate it, and I just don't understand them."

She turned toward me, her eyes sparkling with understanding.

"L.A. is just so full of possibility," she said.

"What's possible here for you?" I asked. "What drew the girl out of the country to the big city?"

Darkness washed over her face, and she broke our gaze, turning back to the ocean.

"Oh, you know, same as anyone who wants a change of scenery."

I reached down, cupping her chin. "What are you running from, Belle? I'd like to know, and...to help if I can."

I hadn't known her long, it was true. But if she couldn't share the very thing that had motivated her to come to L.A., no matter how good or bad it had been, I'd be extremely disappointed. I demanded honesty, even when it hurt.

But I quickly wondered if I'd pushed her too far. She continued staring at the horizon, and her voice shifted to a robotic monotone. "It was my ex-husband. A man I'd been with for ten years. I *had* to leave. Or I would have died. And California was the farthest I could go on the money I had."

Fuck me if that wasn't a serious gut punch. All I wanted was to protect this woman. I knew in an instant that if anyone tried to hurt her, I'd mess them up. I really would.

"Belle, I'm so sorry."

She nodded stiffly and then turned to me as the color came back to her face.

"What about you? How'd you end up in L.A.? How'd you end up an escort?"

"After I graduated from high school, I couldn't get out of town fast enough. My folks, they loved the military, still do, but I hated on-base housing that was always drafty and smelled of the last family's dinners. There was no place for me there if I wasn't going to serve."

Belle nodded, and we started walking toward the trailhead, rocky ground crunching under our feet.

"The minute I arrived in L.A., after a bus ride that took several days and introduced me to quite the freak show of American people, I knew it was the place for me."

"How'd you know?" she asked.

Good question.

"I'm not completely sure I can put it in words. But I felt there was opportunity here, just like you said. It's like it was in the air, as though I could breathe it, smell it, taste it. Sometimes I still think I can, that's how good I feel about being here. I just knew, every morning as I woke up, that if I worked hard enough, I could make my dreams come true."

I caught her hand again as we hiked along the fire road. Her fingers were lost in my big paw, but they were strong and warm.

"I was scrambling when I first arrived, no lie. And then I met Zenia when I was parking cars. She brought me into The Agency and supported my acting ambitions from the start. Everyone should have a Zenia in their life," I said.

I stopped and looked directly at Belle. "I'm sorry I left the other night without saying goodbye."

She was quiet. "Yeah, well. I got your note."

Ouch.

"I'm sorry. We're not supposed to stay the night with clients unless it's...well, pre-arranged. I should have just stayed. It would have been awesome."

She shrugged. "It's okay. I mean, I was disappointed, but it's all good."

Shit. The last thing I wanted to do was hurt this woman. She'd been through enough, already. And while she tried to put on a brave face, I'd made a shitty mistake.

I stopped walking and pulled her to me. It was just the two of us on the wide-open trail, with mountains in one direction and the ocean in the other, all covered by a cloudless, blue sky.

Perfect. Everything was perfect.

I lowered my face to hers, lightly brushing against

her warmed-by-the-sun skin. She smelled amazing—just simple soap and clean girl. Exactly how I liked it. Her breath was warm on my cheek, and she gasped when I grabbed her hair.

It was a dance. That's what it was. A dance to build tension, so that when we couldn't wait any longer, our need would be explosive.

Shit, *my* need already was explosive. And my dick was getting harder by the second.

I lowered my lips to hers, and they were even more delicious than I remembered. Soft, and full, pliable but confident. They slowly let me in, and we explored each other for I didn't know how long, right there in the middle of a canyon fire road.

I ran my hands down her back until I could grab fistfuls of her lush ass. When I dug my fingers into her cheeks and pulled her against my erection, she moaned as I pressed against her stomach.

"*Now* it's all good," I corrected her as I pulled back. "And may I say, Christ you're hot."

Several shades of pink washed over her face, lit up by a smile that about knocked me over.

"Well. You're not so bad yourself," she said.

I pushed her braid aside and went to town on her neck, which was warm and just beginning to perspire under the heat of the day. I passed my lips over her flesh, and her breath quickened when I stroked her nipple through her shirt. I'd only enjoyed a small part of her the other night, and I wanted more. A lot more.

But voices startled us out of our reverie, and a group of hikers giggled discreetly when they caught us. Belle and I moved to the side of the fire road to let them pass, and they smiled at us knowingly and apologetically. Who couldn't relate to needing to kiss someone so badly, you just stopped wherever you were and took care of business?

We walked in silence for probably a half hour, holding hands and lost in thought. Quail and lizards darted across our paths, and other critters made the brushy shrubs lining the fire road shake with their quick movement.

"Would you like to get out of here?" I finally asked, ready to explode. "I think it might be time to be alone."

"Yeah. Let's do it. C'mon."

She pulled me by the hand, and we ran back to my car, passing the hikers who'd just passed us.

"Have a good day," one of them yelled after us.

Oh, we planned to.

CHAPTER 12

BELLE

We got back to the Caddy after our aborted hike—we'd raced, actually, and Xander had let me win. It was all I could do to keep my hands to myself. I wanted to feel him, every inch of him, and have him do the same to me. I nearly asked him to pull me into the back seat but knew a better time could be had at home.

Damn. And I barely knew the guy.

"Where to?" he asked, as he turned the car back down the mountain toward the Pacific Coast Highway.

The thought of returning to my crappy little strip mall apartment depressed me for a moment, but Xander didn't seem to think less of me for it, so what the hell.

"My place?" I suggested.

"Or mine," he offered, reading my tone.

"Where do you live?" I asked, relieved. Maybe I'd just gotten lucky, but Xander seemed to know what I needed and wanted to make sure I got it.

"Actually, not far from here."

He glanced over at me, and my pulse picked up, that familiar tingling between my legs returning. I wanted to go home with this man, see where and how he lived, and to learn more about him. Actually, I wanted to learn *everything* about him.

Although, so far I liked what I had seen. A lot. And it was all hot as hell.

"Really? Lucky you."

"Yup. Right down the hill here, in Malibu."

No. Freaking. Way.

"Oh my god, I love Malibu. It's amazing. You're so lucky."

"I do feel lucky to live there," he said, bringing my hand to his lips for a kiss. "Actually, I'm lucky for a lot of reasons, baby…"

Holy shit. He called me baby. Todd had never used endearments, except for when he called me *bitch*.

The fucker. There he was again, weaseling his way into my head, and my day. But this time, I told myself, I wouldn't let him. I couldn't. He had no part of my life anymore and certainly did not deserve to be in my head while I was driving down a mountain with Xander, who was a real man. Someone who didn't have to put others down to make himself feel big.

Any thoughts of my ugly past slipped away when we arrived at Xander's. It wasn't one of those places you easily saw from the beach, where people had multi-level balconies providing a variety of ocean views. His house was tucked one street back, which was actually better, in my opinion. He was on a quieter street, and because the house was built on a grade, actually *overlooked* the houses that were right on the sand.

"How did you get a place like this?" I asked, wandering around, my mouth hanging open. His house was modern and decorated a bit sparsely for my taste, but it reeked of expensive furnishings and was just as masculine as he was. To top it off, a friendly kitty appeared out of nowhere and rubbed on my bare legs.

God, what he must have thought of my little shit-hole of an apartment?

"A lot of work, and a lot of luck," Xander admitted. "I squirreled away every cent I could from my escort work, and I taught myself a lot about investing. I had a few investments that paid off, and I cashed out at the right time. On top of that, Zenia told me about this place coming on the market early on, and I was able to snap it up before a bidding war took off. I have a tenant in a lower-level apartment who has his own entrance."

"You've got it all figured out, don't you?" I asked as he put his arms around me.

"I don't know if I have anything figured out. There are some days I don't know if I'm doing it right or not.

But there are some things I do know." His eyes gave me a hint, and I ran my hands up his strong back. If I didn't watch it, I'd be tearing his clothes off. Actually, that might not have been a bad idea. The ache between my legs was getting more intense by the moment.

"What do you know? What kinds of things?" I asked in a teasing voice.

"I know that you're very beautiful, despite what you think. I know that your light brown eyes sparkle, and for the past few nights I've dreamed of having you naked in my bed. And I know that, right at this moment, having you here is perfect, and in fact, one of the smartest things I've ever done."

His words warmed me all the way through, and I nuzzled my nose against his neck, with a deep inhale. God he smelled good. Not cologne-y, but just clean with a bit of the day's perspiration.

He lifted my T-shirt off, and slipped down my hiking shorts. I threw off my sports bra and boots, and he took a step back to look me over where I stood in nothing but my thong panties.

"Beautiful. Just beautiful."

Goose bumps exploded across my skin, and my nipples tightened.

"Thank you," I said, as I reached for the button on his shorts. But before I could make quick work of his clothes, he'd picked me up and deposited me on a velvet sofa facing a huge sliding glass door, which in turn overlooked the ocean.

The ocean! In plain, unobstructed view!

The place was flat-out insane. As were the hands he ran all over my body.

A completely self-made man, as humble as they came. Smart, insightful, and sensitive, right there before me, in his house on a freaking beach.

Was I dreaming? Because it sure as hell seemed like it.

I leaned back on the sofa and watched while he kicked off his dusty boots and yanked his T-shirt off over his head.

Oh. My. God.

Even though we'd been intimate a few nights before, I realized I'd not seen him shirtless, and that was a damn shame. And while I was about to see him in even less clothing—I was almost shaking with need—I couldn't take my eyes off his ripped abs and rock-hard chest. His pierced nipples, something I'd never seen before, called me to explore, and I suddenly wondered if I could tug on them without hurting him. The most impressive part, though, was the crazy tattoo of wings that splayed across his chest, begging for my finger-nails. A perfect V of muscle disappeared into the waist-band of his hiking shorts, as did the long thin line of blond hair that descended from his belly button. As if to mar his perfection, there was a tiny little scar on his stomach extending about three or four inches long. But even that managed to be perfect.

He caught me staring like a hungry little puppy as he stood before me, thumbs hooked into his shorts, an amused expression on his face.

"You okay?"

"Um. Yes," I mumbled.

He pushed his shorts down to his ankles and kicked them aside. There he stood before me, stunning in his unselfconscious nakedness, his hard cock glistening with precum.

Naughty boy. He'd not been wearing underwear. And that huge hard-on of his reached to his belly button and bounced against his tummy.

I didn't know where to start, but I did know I was on the verge of losing my mind. From where I sat on the edge of the sofa, I leaned forward and reached for his erection, running my hand from the head to his balls and back up again. His girth was too wide for my grip, and I opened my fingers even further to run my thumb over the head, where I pulled a drop of his precum to my tongue.

"Mmmm," I murmured. It wasn't a lie—he was sweet and tangy, and I wanted more.

"God, your hand feels nice."

I glanced up to find him smiling. He shook out my braid and ran his fingers through my hair, lolling my head around while I laughed.

Getting back to my task at hand, I marveled that I

was inches from the most beautiful cock I'd ever seen —not that I'd seen that many in the flesh. But still.

I scooted to the edge of the sofa to get closer, and using both hands, steered it toward my lips. Not much of it would fit in my mouth, but I wanted to see what I *could* do with it.

My ex had always told me I was terrible at blowjobs, but most everything he'd ever told me had been uttered with an edge of cruelty to shake my confidence. Nice guy, huh?

And he'd been wrong. About so many things.

So this was my first chance to really, truly prove myself, and enjoy doing so. Because the fact was, I *wanted* to suck Xander. I wanted to take him in my mouth, in that strange mix of submission since he would be taking me, later. In my mind, it was the height of sexiness.

I stretched my tongue to the tip of his erection to experience his salty tang once again. I'd never liked that sort of thing before, but this time I found myself ready to beg if necessary. I slipped my lips over his swollen head, and he released a long, low groan.

"Fuck, baby. Goddamn…"

I had to credit *YouPorn* with any semblance of technique I might have had. I'd watched a few blowjobs, exclusively for educational purposes of course, mainly because after escaping the ex, I was eager to figure out how to make the most of any sexual experience. I scooped one hand under his balls, and with another on his shaft, took as much of him as I could. I closed my eyes as they watered lightly, and I let him bounce against the back of my throat.

He let out another groan. Good thing we weren't in my apartment, because the whole building would be enjoying our little session.

And the power! How amazing it was to make someone like him feel so good. His growls sent vibrations down my spine, and need nearly knocked me over.

I wanted to taste every inch of him, but before I could make him explode in my mouth—like I'd seen on the porn vids—he stopped me.

"Baby, hold on."

I released him and looked up. He chuckled as he wiped away a streak of mascara under my watering eyes, and reached for my hands to pull me to my feet.

"You think you get to have all the fun, darlin'?"

He walked me to the window overlooking the ocean and faced me toward the glass, my back to him, while the cool sea air whispered through the windows and over my skin. He hooked his thumbs in the edge of my thong and lowered it over my ass until I could step out of it.

His fingers worked my breasts, where he pulled my sensitive points until my breath got ragged. His cock pressed against my ass, and his hands wandered down my belly. Then he reached my pussy.

He ran a finger through my wet slit and brought it around to my mouth.

"Taste it, baby. You gotta know how good you are."

I tentatively accepted his finger and was immediately intoxicated with my own essence. It was different from when I'd tasted my vibrator on my solo nights. No, this was intense and heady, with Xander's manly flavor underneath my own excited tang. I loved it, my moans crying greediness as I sucked his fingers dry.

His hand fell back to my pussy lips, where he spread me open to find my hard clit. His fingers circled the small bud, and when he zeroed in on it, my knees shook so hard I had to lean my entire upper body against the window to remain upright. "Fuck... yes, Xander...more, please more..."

He picked up the pace of his stroking, and I dropped my head back, giving him perfect access to my neck. The soft kisses he placed there were in wicked contrast to the pounding he was giving my clit, and I pressed my ass against the hard cock burrowing between my ass cheeks.

An orgasm thundered through me, and I slapped the thick glass in front of me, screaming for more. I grabbed Xander's hand and directed two of his thick fingers inside me, where I craved him most. I lifted one knee to open myself further and rocked against the fingers pistoning me.

He held me through uncontrollable shuddering, then scooped my limp body up and carried me to his bedroom. Through half-closed eyes I glanced around a stark room with long white curtains blowing in the sea breeze.

As soon as he lay next to me, I pushed myself up and swung a leg to straddle his hips.

"Do you have a condom?" I managed in a raspy whisper. I was so desperate I might have considered just taking him uncovered, but Xander was prepared. Nodding, he reached into the nightstand and within moments had sheathed himself.

I ran my fingers through my swollen pussy lips and found I was more than wet enough. I pushed myself up on my knees to notch his hard cock right at my opening and let him enter me an inch.

Christ if he wasn't big, stretching me to the point of pain. But I took a deep breath and lowered myself another inch. If other women could do this, so could I. I might be sore tomorrow, but fuck it, I wanted this man inside me, and with one sure thrust, I was full to the hilt, and on the verge of another crushing orgasm. I held him deep inside, eyes closed. I wanted to remember that moment. Savor it. Treasure it.

He lifted me up, nearly all the way off his cock, and then back down, my breasts bouncing as he grew even bigger inside me. He covered the side of my face with one huge hand, pulling me down to accept my kiss. Even as he plowed the hell out of me, his mouth was tender and humble, which was as mind-blowing as anything else from the last week of my life.

I was so close, my senses focused on him and only him—the way he sounded, the way he smelled, the way he held me as he fucked me with all his might.

With a growl that almost scared me, he forced between gritted teeth, "Come on me, baby, c'mon. Come on me."

And he arched his back, stiffening, to drive as much of himself into me as he could, his head slamming back against the bed. He groaned raggedly while I could only whimper, tremors radiating to the end of every hair on my body. I contracted around his cock as he emptied the last of his semen, and collapsed forward, splayed on top of him, my limp form allowing him to press kisses to my neck.

I lifted my head. "Guess I wore you out."

Xander chuckled and wrapped his arms around my body, kissing the top of my head. "Don't count on it, baby. Don't count on it."

CHAPTER 13

XANDER

Watching Belle's lightly slumbering body, I made a simple yet profound decision. That's all there was to it.

I was freaking in awe of this woman.

Even her snoring was sexy.

I mean seriously, how could someone make snoring sexy unless she was at least partially divine?

Unable to resist, I reached out, stroking a lock of her blonde hair out of her face. The movement woke her, eyes fluttering as she wrapped herself around my heart a little more.

"Hey," she said, looking around the room. "Did I doze off?"

"Yup. It was nice. I was just listening to the ocean. And you."

"Hey, can I ask you a question?"

"Sure, ask away, my Belle," I said.

She propped herself up on one arm, her long hair a mass of tangles. "Do you have other clients coming up?"

Couldn't say I blamed her for asking that. It was fair, and something that she needed to know.

"I do."

Disappointment oozed out of her, like a balloon losing its air.

"*But…*" I added before she could get too deflated.

She frowned. "But what?"

"It's probably not what you think."

"Huh?"

"I have a commitment to take one client, an elderly lady, to the ballet—"

"Is that all you're going to do with her?"

Now, I propped *myself* up on an elbow.

"Absolutely. All we've ever done is gone to the ballet." I let out the chuckle inside me. "She's eighty-seven years old, her children and grandkids are scattered all over the country, and her husband died fifteen years ago. She just wants to spend time with someone doing what brings her happiness."

Her face relaxed.

"That's the way it is with most clients…"

Confusion painted her face.

"And I do have something embarrassing to add to that."

"Yeah?"

"I have a stripping gig coming up."

First, her mouth dropped open. Then she bit her lip. I'll be damned. She was trying not to laugh.

I rolled her over on her back and held her hands above her head.

"You think you can laugh at me?" I said in my best gangster accent.

She struggled to get out of my grip. The laughter continued.

And I loved it.

"You...*strip*?" She couldn't hold it in any longer and full-on bellowed, head thrown back, eyes closed.

I laughed as well. "I guess it is pretty funny. But what I think would be funnier right now is to see how you react when—"

In one swift movement I swiveled her across me. I held her down, one arm pinning her and a hand positioned on her ass.

"Hey, let me up. *Stripper man.*" Peals of more laughter.

"You know, I could make you eat your words. Have you ever been spanked?" God her ass felt good under my open palm. Soft, and full...

"No, no, no. Tell me who you're stripping for."

"It's a fancy birthday party," I told her. "The Agency set it up."

She continued squirming.

"For whom?"

147

She was going to love this. Somehow, some way, my last two jobs for Zenia shared a remarkable similarity.

"For a woman who's turning seventy."

She was silent for a moment and then screamed even louder with laughter.

I brought my hand down on her ass cheek with a loud *smack*.

"Okay, okay, okay, I'll stop laughing. Let me up."

"You promise?" I ask.

It *was* pretty hilarious if you thought about it. The guys at work, especially Sandy and Richard, loved to give me shit about stuff like that. Part of it, of course, was my image. I could be the bad boy but also the nice guy. Versatility was key.

"Hey, my phone's ringing," she said.

I let her wriggle out of my grip and watched her run to the living room for her phone, my handprint bright pink on her jiggling bottom.

I rolled over on my side and watched the last of the sun disappear below the ocean.

"Hello?" she said from the next room. "Hello? Anybody there?"

She came back into the room, phone to her ear.

"Jerks," she said, swiping her phone closed.

"What was that?" I asked.

"I don't know. I've been getting tons of hang up calls. Must be some sort of solicitation. I need to get my number on that *do not call* list."

I jumped out of bed and took her hand. Before I had

another taste of my girl, I had a different desire to take care of.

"I'm starving," I said, leading her to the kitchen.

Her hand was strangely cold, but I put it off as I led her through my living room. Still, when I asked her to grab wine glasses from the cupboard, she fumbled one, and it crashed to the floor. The glass exploded like a bomb, pieces flying everywhere, making us both jump.

"Oh my god, I'm sorry..." She knelt, trying to clean the mess, but the only thing in my mind was the fact that she was barefoot and naked, and surrounded by shards of glass. I at least had flip-flops on.

I rushed over and grabbed her, lifting her into my arms. "Hey, don't do that. Let me get it. You're barefoot, and it's just a glass. C'mere."

I carried her across the living room to the couch again, setting her down when I realized her lip was quivering. In fact, her whole body was shaking. I hooked a finger under her chin and tilted her head up.

"Babe, it's only a broken glass. Seriously, they were like, twenty bucks for the whole set. It's okay."

Leaving her for a second, I hurried to my bathroom where I grabbed one of my robes and a spare set of slippers I'd snagged from some fancy hotel. She immediately wrapped the robe's collar around her neck to stop the shivering.

She sniffled, trying to be brave. "Sorry. Sorry about the glass, sorry for losing my shit."

There was no mistaking the dark in her eyes—it

was a haunting look that angered me. We'd been having such a good time, and someone, somehow interfered.

"What's going on? Talk to me," I said.

She shook her head, turning toward the window and gazing at the ocean beyond as she avoided my eyes.

Then she took a deep breath. "You know I came to L.A. to start over."

"Yeah. But isn't that why everyone comes to California?" I said with a small laugh. If I had a dime for every person I'd met in L.A. who was reinventing themselves, I'd be rich.

"Well, I think what I was trying to leave behind might have followed me. I mean, I...I think my ex might have caught up with me."

"You're kidding."

"I hope I'm just being paranoid," she said in a flat voice, almost as if she were no longer in the room with me. "But the number of missed calls just seems like more than a coincidence..."

"You can handle this, baby. I'm right by your side," I said, tracing the scar on her temple. She'd told me about the origins of the little white line, but I knew there was backstory I'd not yet heard. And that she might never want to share with me.

She turned to me, swallowing, before speaking again.

"My life might be danger."

Holy shit.

"Really?"

"Yeah," she said, nodding. She was terrified, and whether it was true or not, she clearly believed it. She absolutely thought her life was in danger.

"He doesn't know where you are, does he? I mean, you covered your tracks when you left, right?"

She took a deep breath. "I did. But that's not a guarantee that a bad person won't find you."

I pulled my arms more tightly around her, and she buried her face in my neck.

"I am scared all the time," she whispered. "Every day, I get up and check the parking lot before leaving, and I do the same again when going home. I'm always afraid that the next customer coming through the door is going to be Todd, with his manic, enraged grin on his face…his hand open so he can teach me another lesson."

"What can I do?" I had some pretty good ideas already. Dark ones, that involved some of the other things I'd learned in my life.

She pulled back and looked at me. "What you're doing right now. Listening to me. Believing me. Being my friend."

But I wanted to do more. And I was going to.

I arrived at The Agency and ran smack into escort *extraordinaire* Sean. Like me, he'd been with Zenia since the early days, although in comparison I always felt like a minor leaguer. Sean was *the man* and could tell stories that would leave my jaw hanging. If there was a male escort hall of fame, he'd be front and center.

And as good as he was at his trade, over time, he'd taken on more of the day-to-day of running The Agency, as a help to Zenia.

And that wasn't all he helped her with. She liked to try the merchandise when she could, and Sean was all too happy to oblige. It was more than just a casual hook-up for them, though. I could see it in their eyes, and I suspected it would eventually become permanent.

"Sean, dude. Long time." We did that guy hug thing, where you shake with one hand and hug with the other.

"How've you been, brother? I haven't seen you in ages," he said, clapping me on the back.

"I know, right? Like two ships passing in the night."

"Zenia told me about your movie. Congrats." A smile stretched across his face, and he was totally legit. Sean was never one to let success go to his head.

"Thanks, buddy. I appreciate that." I looked around the foyer to see if we were alone. "Hey, do you think there's somewhere we could go to talk privately? I have something I want to ask you about."

He pointed toward the stairs. "Sure. Let's go up to

Zenia's office. She's in Palm Springs at a spa or something like that. Getting her fine-tune on."

I laughed as I followed him. Zenia took good care of herself. And she deserved to. The woman outworked any of us, that was for damn sure.

Sean settled onto the sofa, and I took the swivel chair opposite him. I leaned forward, elbows on my knees.

"Oh boy. Where to start?" I said as Sean got a tumbler of whiskey for each of us. Not a lot, but enough to be...friendly.

"What's on your mind, Xander?"

"Sean. I...think there's something you can help me with."

Hi nodded, sitting back in his chair and sipping his drink. "You know I'd do anything for you, man."

"I have a client—well, actually a friend, who needs some help."

A smile spread across his face. "Is she a client? Or a friend? We know how you are, man."

Busted.

"She *was* a client. But now that I'm easing out of the business, I'm going to be spending more time with her. At least I hope to. And she has a problem that I think you can relate to."

"Yeah? What's that?" Sean, who'd had plenty of experiences in life that wouldn't fit on a normal resume, lifted an eyebrow, intrigued.

"She has someone after her."

Sean sat back on the sofa. "Oh, shit. Not good."

"My thoughts exactly."

His eyes grew dark, and he downed the rest of his whiskey in a single shot. Leaning forward, he tapped his fingers together, his mind already whirling. "My first question is, how bad is it? My second one is, do you really want to get involved? This kind of shit is ugly, and often no one wins."

"I don't know how bad it is, to be honest. But she has a pretty nasty scar, mostly hidden by her hairline, but it's there. Draw your own conclusions. But I do know I want to get involved. I already am."

"Okay," Sean said, letting me make my own decisions. "I respect that. You want me to check up on him?"

"Yes. Does The Agency still have access to the service for running background checks?"

He nodded. "Yeah. Zenia uses it all the time. For clients, new guys, you name it. She knows more about you than you do. What's the guy's name? And what's your girl's name?"

"His name is Todd Thomas. Her name is Belle Thomas. I don't know a lot. She doesn't know I'm snooping. But I know they are divorced now, but she's had some close calls with him. Sounds like a fucking psycho. She's been getting a lot of hang up phone calls, so is starting to freak."

"Okay," Sean says. "I'll be honest, that's not a lot to go on. Thankfully you got the ex's name, so that might give me a decent screen to work with. Let me see what I can find out."

"Thanks, Sean. I owe ya one."

The door to Zenia's office blew open and Sandy came flying in.

"Oh, it's you guys. I knew I heard voices. Are you having a meeting? Without me?" he said, looking from one of us to the other with hurt eyes. "Two studs taking a walk on the wild side without me? Tut, tut!"

"Sandy," Sean said, leaning his head back on the sofa. "You'll never change."

He placed his hands on his hips. "Well. I don't know about that. I just have major FOMO."

Sean and I exchanged glances.

"Did you mean to say major *homo*?" I asked.

Sandy blew me a kiss. "I am a major homo, it's true. But don't tell me you don't know what *FOMO* is."

Sean and I both shook our heads.

"*Fear of missing out,* you idiots." He rolled his eyes.

Sean shook his head, and pointed toward the door. "Now, if both of you could take off, I have a *personal* call to make."

I caught the emphasis in Sean's words, and I appreciated them. Taking a look at my watch, I realized had to get ready for the night's gig.

"Yeah, I gotta head out, anyway. I'm stripping at a seventy-year-old's birthday party."

Sean snorted, and I knew I'd hear more about that later.

Sandy on the other hand wasn't so subtle. "All right. Give 'em what you got, my man. But for heaven's sake, don't give any of 'em a heart attack." He threw his head back and howled.

~

Cheesy as it was, dressing up in my cop stripper uniform was a favorite part of my job, and as I drove up to the Hollywood Hills in the Caddy, wistfulness washed over me.

It would probably be my last gig in the uniform.

But I had a hell of a Halloween costume I could always fall back on. It was as authentic as I could make it without getting in trouble, all the way down to the realistic-looking badge.

I rang the bell to a typical house in the hills. It didn't look like much of anything from the street, just your typical sprawling '70s-style rancher, but I knew the back would open up to a canyon that allowed you to see L.A.'s lights for miles. There would be vaulted ceilings and probably a gorgeous pool that no one ever used.

There was a quiet rustle on the other side of the door before it was opened by a woman with glittering blue eyes, silvery hair pulled back into a ponytail, and a lithe figure under flowy silk pants and tunic.

"Oh. May I help you, Officer?"

Perfect. Just perfect.

I pulled a fake notepad out of my back pocket, flipped through some pages, and started scribbling.

"Good evening, ma'am. Is your name Mrs. Sloane?"

Concern crossed her face, and she glanced back over her shoulder at her friends, who, as soon as she turned back to me, broke out in huge smiles.

"Evening, ladies," I called to them. "Sorry to interrupt."

I turned my attention back on the birthday girl.

"Yes, Officer. I am Mrs. Sloane."

"Um, Mrs. Sloane, there's been a noise complaint. May I come in?"

"Of course." She pulled the door open and let me enter.

Just as I'd thought. The house didn't look all that special from the street, but inside was a spectacular example of midcentury-modern luxury. The entire back of it was glass, and yes, the lights of L.A. shimmered in the background.

"Now, Mrs. Sloane, there are a couple ways we can take care of this."

She frowned and glanced at her friends again, who wiped the smiles from their faces just in time.

"I'm afraid I don't understand. We were just having a quiet evening celebrating my—well, just celebrating."

With my hand on my hips, I took a step toward her so I could look right down on her.

"Mrs. Sloane, are you celebrating?"

"Yes."

"Well, I have a question for you."

"And what is that, Officer?"

She was starting to get annoyed. That was good.

"Why isn't there any music playing?"

"Excuse me?"

Cue *Earth, Wind, and Fire*, courtesy of her friend who'd set the whole thing up.

She looked past me to see which of her friends had turned on the music. But just as she did, I grabbed her hands.

She looked up at me, shocked, but as I began to swivel my hips, her face softened and a smile spread across her face. She understood and was more than happy with her 'birthday gift.'

I danced with the beautiful Mrs. Sloane and each of her friends before the evening was out, over the course of the party removing all my clothes except some silly bikini bottoms that came with the outfit. Jesus, if seventy was what these women looked like, I couldn't wait for all the women of the world to catch up to them.

It had been a nice evening, and after I finished humiliating Mrs. Sloane, the ladies asked me to stay for a drink. But Belle was never far from my mind, and I was eager to see what Sean could learn about her ex.

As I put my fake cop uniform back on and drove away from the hills, I was wishing it were a real uniform; it'd help if I had to pay Todd a visit if and when we found him. But I'd protect my girl, regardless. Even if she did snore every now and then.

I was on the freeway before I realized something and smiled. Belle was *my girl*.

It felt good to say that, even if just to myself.

CHAPTER 14

BELLE

With armfuls of the flyers and other junk I'd cleaned out of my mailbox, I fumbled with getting a key into the lock of my apartment door. It took a few tries, and when I was finally inside, everything I was holding fluttered to the ground as I reached for the light switch and locked the door behind me.

God, did my place look like a dump after that palace Xander lived in. But that was okay. I would keep chugging along with my accounting classes and eventually leave behind the glamour of living over a strip mall, and the constant smell of pizza.

It was strangely nice to be home after having spent the night away, even if my own crib was a crappy little one bedroom. But there was one thing that wasn't quite right.

My heart pounded in my chest, and it got hard to breathe.

Right in the middle of my living room sofa was a baseball cap from my old West Virginia high school.

What the hell?

Where had that come from?

I couldn't have put it there. I mean, I didn't have a ball cap with my high school on it. Did I?

I slowly looked around the apartment. Aside from the cap, nothing else seemed out of place. I ran for my closet, where I had a couple caps hanging from hooks from places like Disneyland, Dodger's Stadium, and some event at work where they'd given us caps with Beverly Hills Motors in gold lettering. But I didn't think I had one from high school. Surely I'd have remembered that. Right?

I lowered myself to the edge of my bed, rolling my lip with my thumb and forefinger as I tried to figure it all out. Sure, I was tired from having spent the night at Xander's, and my thoughts were muddled. Why couldn't I remember something as simple as whether or not I had a cap from my high school?

I clasped my hands together to try to stop their shaking as the room spun around me. I rocked forward and back from my place on the bed, as if the movement would soothe the rupture in my stomach. With a deep breath, I pushed myself to my feet and ventured back to the living room where the strange cap remained on my sofa. Staring back at me.

As if it were in control.

Maybe it was.

Because I was almost sure now... I'd never had a cap like that.

But I knew someone who would.

I dashed to the bathroom and lifted the toilet seat just in time to get sick.

Amazing how much power a little cap could have.

I pulled into the lot at the House of Waffles and ran for the door. I brushed past the server who always waited on me and headed straight for the pay phone down the hall.

"Nina?" I said breathlessly as my best friend from home came on the phone.

"Belle? Is that you?" She lowered her voice. "Why haven't you been calling at your regular time? I've been worried sick."

"God, I'm sorry, Nina. I got busy and just forgot. So much going on with classes...and other things. I promise I won't do it again."

A door closed in the background, and she spoke in her regular voice.

"The kids just left for school. This is a good time. How have you been? Everything okay? I really wish you'd give me a number where I could reach you."

I sighed. "I know, Nina. I really want to give you a

way to reach me, but it's not safe yet. I don't want to put you in danger by knowing any more about me than you absolutely have to."

"I know, I know. So what's up?"

My voice broke. "I'm getting kind of worried, Nina. Something weird happened."

"What?"

"Nina, did we ever have ball caps with the high school's name on them?"

"Hmmm. I don't think so. We had sweatshirts, but that was about it."

My breath caught. I didn't want Nina to hear me upset. "Nina, remember how you told me Todd was away with another woman?"

"Honey, that was something I wanted to talk to you about."

I squeezed my eyes shut.

"Why?" I asked.

Nina took a deep breath on the other end of the line.

"Belle, the checker at the grocery store had told me Todd went away with one of her coworkers. But she was wrong. It was some other guy."

"What do you mean?" It was getting harder to breath in the stuffy hallway, and the pay phone cord wasn't long enough to allow me to sit on the floor. There was nothing within reach except a gross old mop that I didn't dare touch.

"Todd didn't go to the Caribbean. And he hasn't

been seen around town in a while either. Honey, he's just up and disappeared."

"Oh god, Nina," I gasped. "I...I gotta go. I'll call you later."

"Belle, wait—"

But I'd slammed the receiver down, and reached into my purse, which tumbled to the floor in my panic. I crouched as I rummaged for my cell, knocking various items out onto the floor including a tampon and my favorite lipstick. When I'd finally found my phone, I scrolled through all the hang-ups to the most recent call, and tapped *redial*.

Whatever number I was calling rang a good five or six times and then picked up.

The number you've reached has a mailbox that has not been set up. Please check the number and try again.

"Are you okay, miss?"

I looked up to see the server I knew, along with the House of Waffles manager, looking down at me.

"I'm fine. Sorry, I was just looking for something." I reached for the lipstick that had rolled to the other side of the hallway and stood, bashing my head on the pay phone's frame.

"*Shit!*" I cried, as tears sprung to my eyes.

"Oh, be careful there, miss," the manager said. "Did the same thing to my knee about six months ago, and I swear—"

"I'm sorry. I'm sorry. I'm leaving now," I said, brushing past them and hustling for the door.

"Miss, is there something we can help you with—"

The second I was in my car, I pressed *lock* on the doors, and sank down in my seat. I scanned the parking lot in my terror, and then as far as I could see in every direction.

I was in danger.

Or maybe I wasn't. How the hell could I know?

Shit. I was already fifteen minutes late for work. I pulled into traffic, looking frantically for any sign of Todd. But it seemed like, at least at that moment in time, the most dangerous thing around was *me*. My eyes were still watering from that smack on the head, and my heart was racing a mile a second. If I didn't find a way to calm down, I'd cause a traffic accident or mess myself up some other way.

So I slowed down and made my way to work. I was chill, at least until I got in the door.

"Jackie!" I ran across the showroom floor. "Jackie, listen!"

"Oh hey, sweetie. How come you're late?" she asked. "I mean, it's no biggie, you're usually on time—"

"I gotta talk to you," I said, throwing off my jacket and stuffing my purse behind the reception desk. "Is Ted in?" I looked around, trying to assess any potential penalty for being late.

"No, he's off today, remember?"

"Oh, right."

I buzzed the girls in service and asked them to keep covering the phones for me for a few more minutes.

I beckoned Jackie closer. "Something's up," I said.

She leaned toward me. "What the hell do you mean? Is it what I think it is?"

I looked around. "It might be. I've been getting hang up calls on my phone, and there was a strange hat on my sofa when I got home."

Her hand flew to her mouth while her face drained of color. "We need to call the police. Belle, we cannot mess around with this," she said in a firm voice. "You gotta treat this shit as real from minute one."

My voice cracked. "Do you think it's him, Jackie? How could he have found me?"

It was getting hard to breathe.

"I don't know, sweetie, but people have their ways. I'm calling the cops for you," she said, reaching for the desk phone.

But I grabbed her arm, freezing her fingers an inch from the phone.

"I've called the police before," I replied, thinking back. Maybe a different department, a different state… but still cops. "They just make things worse."

She shook her head at me. "You can't just sit and do nothing."

I was holding her arm so hard it was leaving marks. "I can't stay today. I need to get out of here. Will you ask the girls in service to cover for me?"

"Sure, honey, but where are you going?"

I grabbed my things.

"I don't know yet. I'll let you know."

"Be careful…" she called after me, but I barely heard her as I rushed for my car.

~

I had no plan as I hit the road, but I guess it was no accident I found myself heading back toward Xander's place. I wanted to feel safe, even if only for a moment. And I knew I'd feel safe with him.

My head reeled with trying to figure out how Todd might have found me. It was incredible. You could cover all your tracks, live a semi-secret life, but if someone really wanted to find you, there was nothing you could freaking do. Not a damn thing.

And I was sick of it.

Sick of being afraid, especially of someone I'd once thought had loved me. And as I covered more ground on my way to Xander's, my fear gave way to anger.

I needed to be pissed. And I was justified. I mean, who did that fucker think he was, terrorizing me? He'd pay, someday, one way or the other—I'd make sure he did. I didn't know how or when, but he would.

When I pulled into Xander's driveway, I looked around to make sure no one was following me.

It was no way to live. *Just no.*

When Xander didn't come to the door, I felt stupid for not calling first. Of course he wouldn't be home. He had a life. So I drove to a little bar I'd passed on the way over, just a couple of blocks from his place. It looked dive-y enough that I figured no one would think I'd ever go in there. Which was exactly why I did.

I had to wait for a moment, once inside, for my eyes to adjust to the bar's dim light. I grabbed a booth in a corner from where I could see the entire place.

A female bartender approached me.

"Can I get you something, miss?" She had black hair to her waist, and tattoos running up her arms. The place probably wasn't even open yet, but something in my face must have kept her from throwing me out into the street.

"Hi. Hey, do you think I could just hang out here for a bit?" I looked around the empty bar. "Maybe I could get some coffee?"

She looked at me like I wasn't the first she'd ever seen in my situation. I guessed when you tended bar in a place like that, you saw a lot.

Nodding, she stuck her pen behind her ear. "Yeah. Sure."

"Thank you. Thank you so much."

I really wanted to just crawl under the table and go to sleep. Instead, I pulled Xander's number up on my phone.

My call went to voicemail. "Xander. I'm in your neighborhood. Something happened, and I didn't know where to go."

I watched the bartender after she'd delivered my coffee as she removed bottles from the shelves behind the bar, cleaned, and returned them to their places. She silently walked by several times carrying cases of beer and other supplies, and as she did, I leaned my head against the hard wooden back of the booth and dozed off.

I never even touched my coffee.

CHAPTER 15

XANDER

"Zenia. How was your spa weekend?" I asked.

Our cell connection broke up, but I knew why she was calling.

"Xander, you asked Sean to run a background check on someone." Her voice was the no-nonsense voice of the businesswoman who ran the best escort business in Los Angeles. By the very nature of her work, she knew people who could get nasty shit done if needed.

"Yeah, I did."

"Xander, why are you running a background check on the ex-husband of one of your clients? That level of involvement is not part of the deal."

Yeah, I'd anticipated that reaction. Background checks require money, resources, and could raise red flags with the wrong people.

"You're right. But I had no choice."

Long sigh. "Xander, you know better. What are you doing?"

I did know better. But this situation was different.

"I understand your concerns, Zenia. I had some myself. Initially. But I'm leaving The Agency, as you know. So that changes things."

"Is this for your client, Belle Thompson?" she asked.

"It is, but she's beyond a client now. There is something about her, Zenia. Something...special, I guess."

I told her what I suspected, and the few scant facts I had. "I should have run it by you, but I didn't think it could wait."

"Be careful, Xander. Please be careful. It doesn't sound like her ex is exactly a nice guy."

"He isn't. That's why I'm doing this. We should know something in the next day or so. I'll let you know what Sean finds."

"Just be careful."

The envelope containing my movie's screenplay was heavy in a very satisfying way, and I held it like it was gold after my agent had handed it over to me in our meeting.

Back in my car, I locked the doors and looked around. Who knows why, but I was suddenly self-conscious. I wanted all the privacy I could get. Like anyone could give a crap about me sitting in my car with a big manila envelope. But still.

I laid the bulky package on the seat next to me, running my hand over the title page as if it were written in braille. My name was scribbled in a corner, along with my role, in a fat Sharpie pen. Finally. Finally, I was holding a full Hollywood screenplay in my hands. A screenplay where I had a role to play, literally and figuratively.

For how long had I dreamed of such a moment?

Sure, I'd been in commercials and had had other tiny roles, but never anything where they'd given me the whole damn screenplay. Usually my instructions were delivered by an assistant-assistant-second director, and consisted of "Go up, ask the blond guy for the keys to room 212, and head up the stairs." This was a huge freaking step.

Yeah, I'd miss The Agency. I'd miss Zenia and the guys, although I supposed I could keep in touch with them. Get together for a beer, once in a while.

And I'd miss a lot of my clients. We'd become friends over time. But, it wouldn't be appropriate to keep up with them over the long term.

Christ, who was I kidding? If all went according to plan, I was going to be slammed with barely any time to myself.

But I *would* find a way to see Belle. There was no doubt about that, I told myself just as my phone vibrated. I'd somehow missed a call from my lovely girl fifteen minutes before. I'd been so excited talking to my agent that I'd disregarded the buzzing in my pocket.

I listened to her message, left in an uncertain and crackly voice. "Um, Xander? I…I need to talk to you…"

The hair stood on the back of my neck, and while my car was hot from the sunshine, I shivered anyway. Tapping *return call*, I sat in my car, my left hand clenched against my thigh. "Please pick up, please pick up…"

She picked up after several rings. "Xander?"

"Where are you? What happened?" I started my car and steered into traffic.

"Oh Xander, I'm afraid. I'm really afraid." Her voice caught.

"Are you home? I'm coming over right now."

"No, no I'm not home. I'm near your house, at the bar down the street. I came to your house and you weren't there."

"All right, stay where you are. I'll be there in forty-five minutes."

While it was hard to picture Belle hanging out in the roughneck bar down the street from my house, I knew she'd be fine until I got there.

It was hard not to slam my foot through the floor-board, and as I sped down the 101 to the PCH, I was so tempted to see just how many horses I could urge out of the Caddy. I wrestled my way through the heavy traffic on Pacific Coast Highway, tempted to blow all the red lights holding me up. But I knew that would do no one any good were I to be pulled over for a traffic violation, or worse.

When I finally reached the bar, I left the Caddy on the street corner and ran inside. Belle was slumped in a booth in the back corner, while the bartender chatted with a couple of burly guys wearing leather vests. She gave me a wary look, but I caught Belle's eye as I approached, and before I knew it, she'd jumped into my arms. The bartender nodded, and I reminded myself in my second of clarity before I focused on Belle to come back sometime to thank her for watching out for my girl.

"Oh my god, Xander, I've been so scared. I'm so happy to see you."

She buried her face in my neck, and I knew the wet I felt was from tears.

I held her at arms' length. She was a mess, and while it wasn't her fault, my voice was rough, and tinged with anger. Anger at whatever had put her in that state.

"What the hell is going on? Are you okay?"

Her eyes were wild with fear.

She glanced around and realized the biker guys had turned in their seats to see what the commotion was about. She straightened up and pulled her shoulders back, wiping her eyes with the back of her hand.

She looked back to me. "I'm fine," she said, throwing a weak smile back in the direction of the bikers. "It's okay, guys, really. He's...he's who I was waiting for."

I pulled her back into my arms. "Okay. I'm here now. I want to hear what's going on."

I threw some bills on the table, and Belle waved at the bartender on the way out. I reminded myself again to come back another time, thank her, and slip her an extra few bucks just for being that sort of person. Not everyone in LA. is willing to look out for a stranger.

I moved my screenplay to the back seat as Belle slid into my car, and when I'd gotten in on the driver's side, I pulled her to me.

"I'm not going to let anything happen to you, you know."

She nodded silently. "Thank you. Thank you so much."

"And if I'm not around to look out for you, I have a lot of friends."

That made her giggle.

"It's good to hear you laugh," I said.

She looked up at me. "That just sounded so gangster. *I knows some people*, and all that."

"I guess it did. But I'm serious. Now, can you tell me what happened?"

By the time we got back to my place, she'd spilled the whole freaky story of a hat appearing on her living room sofa, and then finding out her ex had not been on vacation, but had instead pretty much vanished into thin air.

Shit, I'd be freaked-out, too.

"I don't know what to do. I've been running for so long. I just don't think I can keep going."

"You don't have to. We're going to take care of the situation," I said.

"How? Where are we going?"

"To your place."

"*What?*"

"We're going to your place so you can pick some things up. Then we're coming back to my place. I want you to stay with me."

I glanced over at her beautiful, confused face.

"If you will, that is," I added.

"Oh." Her voice broke again.

I pulled her hand to my lips.

"We're going to straighten this situation out. Until we do, I want to make sure you're safe."

I glanced at her while waiting at a red light. Her eyes were full of tears, which was way better than the terror I'd seen in them just a few minutes earlier.

"I'm embarrassed to have you back in my apartment, after having seen where you live."

I busted out a laugh. "That's about the last thing you should be worrying about right now. You've got bigger fish to fry, and I've seen your bedroom, remember? Besides, you should see where I grew up. Military housing leaves a lot to be desired."

As I pulled up to her building, a plastic grocery bag and an old piece of newspaper blew across the parking lot. It was already early evening, and a flickering streetlamp cast a creepy glow over her big metal front door —the kind of door that *should* have been really hard to break into.

But apparently wasn't.

"You want to wait here while I get some things?" she asked.

Was she crazy?

"No, I am not waiting here. I'm coming in with you. C'mon."

Her hands were shaking as she fumbled with her keys, so I grabbed them from her and got us inside, noting that the latch on the door was not as secure as it could have been.

I entered her apartment first, scanning the living room and kitchen. I was pretty confident in my abilities to take another guy, but the element of surprise was never a fun one to deal with.

"Wait here," I told her quietly. I took a quick look around, checking everything including the bathroom, and then let her come in.

"It's okay. Let's get some of your things."

Belle went straight for her bedroom, and I grabbed the mysterious baseball cap, still on the sofa, and stuffed it in my back pocket to get rid of later.

"You know, baby," I called, "I actually like this place. It's really cozy. Does the job."

She came out with a backpack and an old duffel bag, which I took and slung over my shoulder.

"Thank you." She looked around. "It's not my

forever home. I liked it because it seemed safe and out of the way. Now I'm not so sure."

I looked up and down the hallway as we left. I couldn't put my finger on anything in particular, but something about the place didn't feel right.

"Maybe I should go to a hotel," Belle said quietly as we got into my car.

"What? Is that what you prefer? Over staying at my place?" There was no way I could let her do that. She just needed a bit of convincing. "You'll be safer with me, you know. This isn't about trying to seduce you, or getting laid."

Although if that were to happen, I wouldn't complain.

"I want to make sure nothing happens to you. You've already been through hell and back. I'll even sleep in the guest room if you want the bed to yourself."

"Really?" she asked, her voice hitching. "But...no, you don't need to do that."

I reached to run my finger through another tear running down over her cheek, and brought it to my mouth. Through the saltiness, I tasted her fear, sorrow, and anger.

My girl.

"Your car is back at the bar, right?" I asked.

She nodded.

"Okay. We'll put it in my garage to keep it out of sight."

I maneuvered through the traffic to get back to Malibu, my mind still trying to figure out step two in this whole plan, when Belle tapped me on the arm.

"What's that package on the back seat?"

Christ, in all the excitement I'd forgotten about my damn movie.

"That is the screenplay of the movie I'm going to be in. If you're up for it, maybe you could run lines with me later?" I asked. If anything, it would take her mind off things.

"Run lines. What's that?"

"You know, read through my lines with me," I reply. "Like play the other roles, bounce off my character's lines. Help me memorize them. I mean, I don't think I have that many. But I still have to learn them."

Her voice picked up. "That sounds like fun. I can pretend to be a movie star."

I reached for her hand. "Now you're talking, sweetheart. Shit, you'll probably be a better actor than me."

She laughed—first time I'd heard that in awhile.

"Well, I doubt it. But I can say I *'knew you when,'*" she said.

"That's fine, but I'm hoping you'll *still* know me *when*."

CHAPTER 16

BELLE

Xander's kindness flooded me with a confusing mix of emotions—from shame to overwhelming gratitude and back again. It was all new, accepting that someone believed in me and wanted to keep me safe.

Safe.

That was something I'd like to get used to, like a new normal. I'd not felt safe in so, so long...

I was still shaken to the core over how the mysterious baseball cap might have ended up on my sofa. On one hand, I didn't want to know. And as long as I didn't come out and say it, and as long as it remained a mystery, I didn't have to face the nightmare that was threatening to shatter my carefully constructed denial.

But the reality was, there was only one way that thing could have ended up in my apartment. As much as I would rather have buried my head in the sand and deny or pretend I knew nothing, the fact was, I *did* know. Finally, after sitting in Xander's passenger seat and calming down enough to feel at least temporarily safe, I could say it to myself. He was back.

Todd had somehow found me, gained access to my apartment, and left the hat there to send a message. What message, I had no idea. But I was certain it wasn't intended to be a pleasant one.

I couldn't begin to fathom how the fucker had found me. But it didn't really matter. I'd learned my lesson. And it was a lesson that I didn't think he would have expected.

No more running.

Because running got you nowhere.

And if there was nowhere to run and be safe, there was only one other alternative. Face the problem, head-on. Take care of business. I wasn't exactly sure yet what that might look like, but I had to take care of the problem one way or the other. It would not go away until I did, that much was clear.

After I'd loaded up as many of my belongings as could fit in Xander's car, the ride back to his place was mostly quiet. I don't think we knew what to say, given our newfound alliance, and of course, attraction.

As he drove, I stole glances at his beautiful profile.

The streetlights flashed over his face, leaving him illuminated one moment and in the shadows, the next.

He pulled up next to my VW, across from the bar where I'd hidden, and waited until I was safely in my car. In the few minutes I was driving behind him, rather than sitting next to him, I freakily found myself sinking back into vulnerability. With a growing lump in my throat, I scanned the horizon in every direction looking for danger.

I was sick of it. So, so sick of it.

At his place, he directed me to his garage and closed the door behind us.

"You tired?" he asked as we entered his kitchen.

Was it that obvious?

"I am...exhausted." I followed him down the hallway where I could see the moonlight glinting off the waves, and I wondered how it had gotten so late.

He gestured toward his room. "Why don't you settle into my bedroom? Get comfortable. The robe you wore the other night is on the bathroom door."

I watched him walk away. "Xander?"

"Yes?" he asked, turning to face me.

"Thank you."

He studied me for a moment and nodded. "I'm not going to let anything happen to you."

I opened my mouth to speak, but nothing came out. I mean, what did you say when someone was so freaking amazing? Words seemed so...inadequate.

He continued down the hall toward the kitchen with his screenplay under his arm.

"Xander?"

"Yeah?" he asked again, turning back around.

"Could I have some tea?"

He smiled, and my heart melted a little more. "Sure. Coming right up."

I took a deliciously hot shower, and when I finished, bundled up in Xander's huge white robe. It smelled clean and spicy, just like he did, and I pulled it tighter, imagining his arms around me.

But I didn't have to imagine for long. He was waiting for me with my tea, and a scotch for himself, in the reading chair of his bedroom.

I wrapped my hands around the warm mug and took a deep breath, letting the aroma soak through my head and help me relax. "That shower was just what I needed. And this tea smells like heaven.

He popped up out of his chair. "I'll leave you, then." He landed a soft kiss on my lips and turned toward the door.

"Xander?" I asked for the third time.

"Yeah?"

"I don't want you to sleep in the guest room," I said, summoning up all the courage I had left in me that night. "I want you to sleep here with me. Okay?"

"If you're sure, then okay. I'll be in a bit later. I want to skim my screenplay. You can have some time to yourself...you're safe now."

I took his advice, snuggling into his massive bed and burrowing under the fluffy down comforter after a few sips of my mint tea. I'd forgotten my ratty old pajamas behind at the apartment, which was probably just as well. The sheets were momentarily cold against my bare skin, but by the time I warmed them up, I had fallen into that place right before sleep where your thoughts go wild and anything is possible.

"Belle. Belle, wake up."

It took me a few moments to shake off my dream. I was so confused. Why was Xander shaking me by the shoulder? And where was I? How the hell did the ocean get outside my window?

Oh. The dream…the hat…Todd.

Xander brought his face close to mine, and I remembered where I was.

And why I was there.

"Oh my god, Xander. My dream…he's here. I know he's here," I said, in a shaking voice. "I was running, but a shape was—no, *he* was chasing me."

"Belle, it was a bad dream," Xander reassured me. "You're fine. I'm with you."

I threw myself into his arms.

"Oh my god. It was awful."

"You were making horrible noises. I heard you from the living room. But you're okay now." He stroked my hair, and as he did, the down comforter slipped to my waist. He hadn't expected me to be nude.

He pulled back, his hands on either side of my face, and looked at me. But I wasn't embarrassed. Instead, I felt sexy. And beautiful. I followed his gaze over my breasts and watched the back of his hand stroke one of my nipples, now painfully erect. He looked at me with a gaze that could only be described as hunger, and moving in to kiss me, tightened his fingers on my sensitive point.

"You're gorgeous, baby. And so fucking sexy," he whispered just before his mouth crashed on mine.

I grabbed his head to pull him closer. I couldn't get enough. I wanted to inhale him so he lived in every pore of my body. I wanted him to be my oxygen, and I wanted to be his.

He laid me back on the pillows, and I watched him, one hand behind my head. As he removed his clothes, my gaze traced the splay of hair that narrowed to a line ending at his perfectly shaped cock, which by now was so hard it bounced against his flat stomach. With his clothes strewn over the floor, he pulled the comforter back and climbed onto the bed next to me.

"Turn over," he said in a quiet voice.

Who was I to argue? I flipped over, onto my stomach, eager to feel his touch. On one hand it was odd to be so turned on after being so scared just minutes before, but the distraction was a lifesaver.

"Mmmm, beautiful..." he murmured, running his open palms over the cheeks of my ass.

His touch was so light that goosebumps exploded on my heated skin, a crazy sensation I wouldn't have believed existed if I hadn't experienced it. I couldn't see behind me but felt him swing one leg over my hips so he could straddle me. My legs were held tightly together, wedged between his. His balls tickled the flesh of my behind, as he ran his hands from the nape of my neck to my ass cheeks, which he grabbed by the playful, electrifying handful. I pushed back into him as best I could, hungry for more contact...more anything, really.

Still behind me, he maneuvered the two of us until my legs were spread and he was between them. I was open and exposed, and while I was embarrassed, it didn't last. I felt his gaze burn against my bare pussy, and when he pulled my cheeks open, he saw my asshole, too.

I'd never had anyone take a good long look at my most private parts like he was, and when his hot breath touched me down there, my own started to come hard and fast. I didn't know what he was going to do.

I didn't care. He could have done anything, and it would have been all right.

But I never imagined he'd place his tongue, well, *there*... I mean, I'd seen it in the pornos I'd watched, but those people were paid and would do all sorts of wild things. People didn't really did lick each other down there, did they?

God, I didn't know whether to scream *stop* or ask for more. I was a bundle of emotion, vacillating between mortification and boldness. But when he spread me as far open as he could and tasted me from one end to the other, I reached back and spread myself further, burrowing my face in the pillows to muffle my screams.

With his hands now free, he notched a finger at the opening of my pussy, teasing me with featherlight strokes. I wiggled closer so he could fill me, and in seconds, his fingers were buried to the hilt. I didn't know how many he was using, and it didn't matter. He pistoned me until I shuddered with convulsions, coming loudly on his hand.

"That's a good girl," he growled.

"Oh Xander. Fuck me like that. Fuck me harder," I screamed, needing the release as much as I needed air.

In an instant, he flipped me over, still thrashing from my orgasm. In all the excitement, I hadn't noticed him roll on a condom. He flipped to his own back and held his cock with one hand.

"C'mon. Climb on top."

Still weak, I pushed myself up until my legs were on either side of his hips. I took a deep breath and got my feet under me so I was effectively crouching over him. He stared at my open pussy with a beatific smile and steered himself toward my opening.

I lowered myself onto him just an inch or so. While he'd opened me and got me nice and wet with his fingers, there was no way they could prepare me for the knob that was the end of his cock. I let myself adjust to his girth and lowered myself some more.

"Look at you, baby. Taking my cock into that pretty pussy. It's so good. So good."

He dropped his head back onto the pillows and grimaced from the sensation of being buried inside me.

When he was completely seated, I leaned back, my hands on his thighs, for balance. I rolled my hips up and down on his hard dick with such a fury I couldn't even think. All I could do, really, was feel.

I continued bucking, and Xander's hips rose to meet mine. We slammed into each other until we were near exhaustion, when he threw his head back and began to roar.

"Goddamn, baby, I'm coming…fuck yeah," he shouted.

I flipped from my feet to my knees and leaned forward to press against him. The coarseness of his chest hair chafed my sensitive nipples, and the pain from that, and the pounding in my pussy, threw me into a red-hot orgasm that burned through every inch of my body. I buried my mouth in his neck and screamed as he pulled me closer and pumped the last of his cum.

We gradually got our breaths back, and I moved off him, removing the condom and knotting it at the end.

He wrapped his arms around me, and I pressed against his chest.

I fell asleep thinking of ways to keep that day from ending.

But of course it had to end. Everything had its end, didn't it?

CHAPTER 17

XANDER

Until I knew more about what Belle was up against, I wasn't going to risk leaving her alone. And while I couldn't be with her around the clock, I was doing my best to make sure she was safe at all times. That included taking her to and from work.

"I really don't mind driving myself. I'm sure it's fine," she said as she made coffee in my kitchen.

She looked damn good in my kitchen, I might add. She was wearing one of my undershirts, her breasts filling the cotton, with her new pajama shorts just barely peeking out from underneath the hem.

I took the cup she'd offered me and ran my fingers through her bed-head hair. "I know you don't mind. But at least for now, let's play it safe. Just give it a bit of time. We'll see how things shake out."

I hadn't told her I was having a background check done on her ex. It was sneaky of me, and I did feel a bit badly about it, but for now, I needed to follow my instincts. Before I could really protect her, and hopefully turn the situation she was in around, I needed to know what I was up against.

I mean, was the guy just an egotistical asshole who couldn't stand being left by his wife?

Or an all-out psycho?

Were we talking some tough-guy posturing and a restraining order, or would I have to get some of Zenia's problem-solving friends involved?

Hopefully the background check would shed some light on that and more. I'd know in the next few days whatever info Sean had been able to dig up.

I pulled the Caddy up to Beverly Hills Motors and looked around the parking lot. It was tricky being there, because there were always people milling about, along with their cars. And there were too many doors. No way to check everyone coming on and off the lot.

"Promise me you won't go anywhere alone? Stick with your friend Jackie until I pick you up at the end of the day, okay?" I asked, knowing at least Jackie knew the truth, more or less.

Belle nodded, bravely. But I wasn't fooled.

"I promise. Everything will be fine. Seriously," she said, planting a soft kiss on my mouth, then exiting my car.

I watched until she was inside.

Something felt off. But I couldn't very well follow her into work or to her classes, could I?

As she moved across the large showroom, I could see her fishing through her purse. She pulled out her cell, and after what I guess were a couple hellos, she looked at the screen, shook her head, and swiped across it to hang up her call.

Another hang-up? Shit.

In the couple days she'd been staying at my place, I'd seen her pick up a few calls where no one was on the other end of the line. When I asked her about them, she brushed it off, saying it was probably just a wrong number. But I knew better.

And she did, too.

I drove across town to The Agency, and when I arrived, I went straight to Zenia's office.

"Hey, beautiful," I said to Zenia, giving her a kiss on the cheek. "Looking stunning as always."

"Sweetie, so good to see you," she said. "And thank you. You never fail to make me want to look good."

"How was the spa?" I asked, settling into a white leather chair opposite her desk. She'd never told me last time, and I was genuinely curious. Might be a nice getaway for Belle, when all the dust had settled.

She rolled her eyes and smiled. "Divine. I mean, total perfection."

"You look relaxed."

"I am. Or should I say, I *was*? I'm a little freaked about your leaving. Will you find a bit of time to spend with your replacement, Will, while he comes up to speed? Please?" she asked.

"Of course. In fact, that's along the lines of what I wanted to talk to you about."

"Really? What's going on?"

I looked out her office window to Melrose Avenue several stories below.

"Zenia, I know you have me set up for a couple more dates, and that one of them is taking Mrs. S to the ballet. But I can't do it."

The expression on her face morphed from pleasant to cold. It was amazing how protective she was of her business. It didn't matter how much she liked you. But I guessed that if I looked at my business like it was my baby, I'd feel the same.

She leaned across her desk and folded her hands together.

"What is going on?" she asked.

"I'm not available for any more dates. It's that simple. I'll be able to give pointers, coach my replacement, but...that's it. Physically, emotionally, I just can't do it in good conscience. It wouldn't be fair to you...or her."

She was a smart woman. She could read between the lines.

After a long silence, she said, "All right. I'll get someone to cover for you. But I hope you know what you're doing Xander. I really do."

I stood to leave. "It's all good, Zenia. I'm happier than I think I've ever been."

She raised her eyebrows, which was to be expected. Everyone in L.A. was cynical, and no one more so than Zenia.

"I'm glad for you, Xander. Things are really coming together for you. Just remember to invite me to your first movie premiere."

"You bet. You're first on my list. You know that."

I left her smiling just like she'd been when I'd arrived.

And I was on to my next task.

"Sean, thanks for meeting me," I said to my colleague and friend. The restaurant wasn't fancy, but the tacos were some of the best around, and more importantly, I knew Sean and I could have some privacy.

He slid into the booth. "Good to see you, buddy. How's things? You look like you forgot to shave," he said with a laugh. "You going metro on me now?"

I automatically reached for my scratchy beard. "Yeah, I know, I know. It feels weird as shit. But I have to grow it for the movie."

Sean nodded, his eyes lighting up. "Dude. You must be so psyched about that."

"You don't even know. I'm still freaking amazed that it's happening."

We were silent while the waitress dropped off our beers.

"So, how's your girl? The one who was a client?" he asked.

I nodded slowly. "She's hanging in there. She's scared though. I just met with Zenia to say I'm not seeing any more clients."

"Whoa. How'd she take it?" he asked.

"She wasn't doing backflips, that's for sure. But I'm pretty sure she's not holding it against me. I've been good to her. She knows it was time for me to move on. I'll be honest, part of me feels like shit for not tapering my work off more gradually. But I had to do it this way."

"All right," Sean said, raising his beer in a toast. "Gotta respect that. A man knows when he's done."

We ate our tacos in silence. I felt better, reassured that maybe I could have future friendships with The Agency.

When we were mostly done, Sean spoke up again. "So, I got the background check you needed."

"Yeah? How's it looking?" I asked.

He looked at me hard. "Dude, you sure you want to get mixed up in this shit?" He shook his head. "I took a look, and it's nothing to read before bed."

"I already am mixed up, my friend. There's no turning back."

"All right." He reached into his backpack and pulled

out a thin envelope. "Here. Go through this when you have the chance."

I slipped it onto the bench seat next to me, where it was out of view.

"Okay. Any highlights you care to share?"

He leaned forward slightly and lowered his voice. "I think you should run in the opposite direction. That's what I would do, anyway."

"You know that's not how I roll."

"Point taken," Sean said. "Okay, this guy I ran the check on, Todd Thomas, is bad news. Did you know he put his ex—your new girl, apparently—in the hospital last year?"

I pushed my plate away. I was suddenly sick to my stomach.

"I'm not surprised to hear it."

"Apparently, it might not have been the first time. He may have broken her arm earlier, too, but it was never proven or charged. But after the last incident, she walked out. He didn't take it well. She notified the cops. But before she could get a restraining order, not that that would have done any good, he got his hands on her. And it wasn't pretty. She ended up with a fractured cheekbone and several lacerations," he said. "I'm glad I didn't get pictures of that, honestly."

Jesus. This was no run-of-the-mill typical piece-of-shit ex. This guy was fucking bad news. Psycho bad news.

"And he got away?" I asked.

"Apparently. He's a clean-cut professional. Super straight looking, and in the town—the small town, apparently—he had connections. Old-boy network sort of connections. He talked himself out of any real trouble."

No wonder Belle was terrified.

"Do we know where he is now?" I asked.

"Yeah. This is where I had to push the limits of what my contacts would do for me. But you've always done me a solid, so I wanted to go all the way. Looks like the fucker's a real pro—when he ghosted, he ghosted real good. But, he did slip and use a credit card a couple weeks ago. Guess he needed a rental car and couldn't get one without a card. He had no idea just how helpful using that card would be. To anyone looking for him, that was."

I glanced at my watch and threw some money on the table. "This is good stuff, Sean. I seriously owe you."

He smiled and shook his head. "You don't owe me a damn thing. But try and take care of that girl. She must be something special for you to be putting yourself out the way you are."

I paused and nod. "She is something special. Very special."

The next day, after I'd dropped Belle off at work, I headed to the studio for my first day on set. My lovely girl had run lines with me for hours the last couple of nights, which had been good for us both—it took her mind off her worries and helped me memorize my shit. All I had to do now was show up and dazzle them.

"Xander. Wonderful to see you," the director crooned. She also pushed her tits together, like that was somehow part of her normal greeting style.

Christ, did she really think she was being seductive?

"Good to see you." I waved across the room at the starlet I'd kissed at the audition. She looked up and smiled, obviously remembering who I was.

"Xander, my assistant will show you to makeup. We're going to rehearse the fight scenes today. Are you up for that?" she asked.

"Absolutely."

About an hour later, I stood under unbearably hot lights with the guy I'd be fighting against, and our coach, whose job it was to make it *look* like we were kicking the shit out of each other when we really weren't.

"You guys ready?" the coach asked. "Listen, this is an art. It'd be easier if I just let you two beat each other to a pulp...but that's not how we make films. Just sell the moves right, and let the effects team do their magic with the rest."

The guy I was matched with was a stand-in for the movie's star, who had no fighting background. I guess when you got to be a household name, they didn't care what you could or couldn't do as long as you could sell movie tickets.

So my 'enemy' and I sparred for a while, with the coach calling out instructions. Just when I thought we were both getting the hang of what I was calling 'play fighting,' my opponent and I misjudged how close we were, and his boot landed smack in my ribs. I went down, wondering if I'd ever be able to breathe again. This wasn't like getting kicked when sparring. *Then* I knew what was coming. This was unexpected, and undefended.

And fucking painful.

My eyes filled with tears, that's how much agony I was in. I lay on the floor in a fetal position with my arms wrapped around my body for protection. Several folks were hovering over me, while the coach kneeled down by my side.

"Xander. Xander, talk to me."

At first all I could do was groan, but after a minute or so I got my voice back. "Yeah," whispered hoarsely.

"Can you get up? C'mon, let me help you up."

I extended him my hand from the uninjured side of my body, and he pulled me to my feet. I was getting my breath back but couldn't straighten up all the way.

"Let's get you an X-ray."

"No. No, I don't need one. I'm feeling better already," I said. It was only a half lie. I knew that if they really found something wrong with me, they might find a replacement. I'd be shit out of luck.

"You sure, Xander?" the director asked, rubbing her hand up and down my arm. As long as she didn't touch my ribs…

"I'm okay. Really. Just knocked the wind out of me," I said. "And boots suck."

That got a few laughs, and the director smiled. "Okay, everybody. Let's call it a day on the fight scenes. We'll pick this up again tomorrow. Xander, why don't you rest a bit and head home when you are up to it?"

"Absolutely. Sorry to mess up the day."

The coach led me over to a sofa and helped me sit.

He lowered his voice. "Sure you don't want an X-ray? You could be really hurt."

"No, man. I'm good. Just gotta get my breath back," I said.

"I gotcha. It's smart to play it down. The studios are scared to death of being sued. They'll drop you like a fly if you are really injured. At least until you've got a bankable name."

I looked at him. "I appreciate that. Thank you."

"All right. Take some Advil and put a heating pad on it." He patted me on the shoulder and took off.

I'd better fucking be okay. I might be fake fighting at the studio, but I could have some real fighting to do if things went down the way I thought they might.

CHAPTER 18

BELLE

How the hell did I get from my nasty little strip mall apartment to a house in Malibu with a view of the ocean, that just happened to be owned by one of the most handsome men I'd ever laid my eyes on?

Who, by the way, I'd paid to take me on our first date, and who was now on his way to becoming a movie star?

Life was truly strange.

With his cat on my lap, I looked around Xander's living room one more time to make sure I wasn't dreaming and then returned my gaze to the waves smashing on the shore. One after the other, they just kept coming. The effect was mesmerizing, and I hadn't felt so relaxed since…well, I couldn't remember.

I'd hoped Xander would have been able to relax the whole weekend after having had his ribs kicked in. But there it was, Sunday, and he had to go to the studio for something. What, I wasn't sure. He hadn't been clear either, just telling me the set was hollering for him, and apparently he was needed ASAP.

I guessed acting, at least when you were starting out, was not a Monday through Friday gig.

Not that working in a car dealership was limited to weekdays—it's just that my schedule only included one weekend per month, and even then I got paid overtime. All that extra money I socked away in the bank, vowing to leave it untouched except in case of a serious emergency.

I needed that sort of flexibility in my life. Until Xander came into it.

But honestly, were things really that different now? I mean, sure I had a better view, at least at the moment. But was I safer? Was I rid of my psycho ex?

It sure didn't feel like it.

I padded around Xander's place, the cat hot on my trail, both of us restless as hell for different reasons. Yeah, I had some accounting homework to do, but I couldn't seem to concentrate, while he just wanted a human to put a few treats in his bowl. I flipped around the cable channels and then sorted through the romance books I'd started ages ago, but nothing was sticking. What I really wanted to do was run over to my apartment and get some more clothes and one of my forgotten textbooks.

But I couldn't do that. I'd promised Xander I wouldn't go near the place without him. Honoring that was the least I could do.

Right?

But the more I thought about it, the more I realized I needed that damn book. Picking up extra clothes would just be a bonus.

And Xander wouldn't be home for several more hours. I could just zip over there and back.

He'd never know. And I'd be careful. Really careful.

I threw on some leggings and a sweatshirt, tossed my phone in my bag, and looked out the front windows for anything strange. There were no cars or people in sight. Guess Sundays in Malibu were pretty slow. I tucked my hair into one of Xander's baseball caps, pulled on a large pair of sunglasses, and headed to the garage where my little VW was hiding out.

I headed for Pacific Coast Highway in my sort-of disguise. It was a stunning day with a bright blue sky, the mountains on my left, and the glittering ocean on my right. How could so much physical beauty be infused with such pain and fear? I just didn't get it.

As I closed in on my neighborhood, I checked my phone to see if Xander might have been looking for me. I didn't want him to know I'd left his house, so had to be sure to answer, should he call.

And don't you know, my phone had one percent of the battery left and was fading fast. I'd taken the charger out of my car earlier, and now it was at Xander's house.

Fuck, fuck, fuckity fuck.

If he called, I'd be so busted. I had to take care of business really quick and get the hell back.

When I arrived at the shitty strip mall I called home, I drove around the block a few times to case the place. I saw nothing unusual. No one sitting in their car for no apparent reason, and no strange characters walking around. The pizza joint downstairs had a couple of people in it, and the owner, who lived upstairs just like I did, was behind the counter, tossing dough in the air for show. Things seemed pretty calm in my crappy corner of the world.

Maybe it was just as well my phone had died. It'd be best that Xander couldn't actually reach me, to be honest.

I got out of my car and ran into the pizza shop.

"Belle," the owner said. "Long time no see."

"I've been busy. Staying over at a friend's. Hey, could I get a soda?"

"Coming right up." He handed me my favorite, a Diet Coke, and I tossed two dollars onto his counter.

"How have things been here? Pretty quiet?" I asked.

"Oh, you know how it is. We'll never sell like gangbusters in this location, but we make enough to get by. The takeout service has been strong."

I nodded and took a sip from my giant soda. From

what I could tell, the shop had been there twenty years, and for twenty years the owner had probably been bitching about the same things.

I stalled. "Good. Glad to hear it. Anyone strange coming by?" I turned and looked directly at him. "Anyone asking for me?"

He frowned for a millisecond, followed by an understanding that crossed his face.

"No, Belle. Not that I've seen anyway. You in some kind of trouble, sweetheart?" he asked.

I considered telling him. But I couldn't. That might put him in danger.

"No," I said, shaking my head. "It's all good. It was nice seeing you. Thanks."

I'd wanted the soda, but the main reason I'd gone into the pizza shop was to buy some time and scope out the parking lot from a different perspective. But all was well. I was probably just being paranoid.

As I approached, I had the key to my apartment building in my hand, poised to slip right into the lock, and my soda in the other. I didn't want to be fumbling with my keys, trying to get the damn door open. That would leave me too vulnerable.

But I got right into my building. My musty, dingy building. With the big metal door shut behind me, the place was a toss-up between a prison and a safe house. Well, I *had* felt safe —until recently.

I grabbed my mail and ran up to my apartment, locking the door behind me as soon as I was inside.

All was exactly as I'd left it, with the mysterious cap out of sight—I'd seen Xander stuff it into his back pocket. I grabbed a phone charger from one of my kitchen drawers and plugged my phone in for a little more juice.

Using a garbage bag as luggage, I began pulling clothes from my dresser. When I gathered about as much as I could possibly carry, I dug through the accounting books on my nightstand and grabbed the one I needed most, as well as my phone, which now had about a ten 10 percent charge. It was better than nothing, and if I were careful about using it, it would last for a little while. As I headed for the door, I realized I'd left my soda on the counter. I ran back to get it.

With full arms, I looked up and down my hallway for any signs of life. But the place was dead quiet, with nobody to be seen. I mean, who would stay inside a crappy place like that on a beautiful, sunny day in L.A.? Nobody, that's who. My neighbors were undoubtedly at the beach or at a park somewhere.

I descended the stairs carefully, but on the last step lost my footing. I recovered from my stumble, none the worse for wear, but in the process of grabbing the hand railing to steady myself, my soda had gone flying. Diet Coke, ice, a large cup, lid, and straw now littered the bottom steps and the floor in front of the door.

Shit. I couldn't leave that there. The next person to come into the building would surely wipe out.

I thought for a moment, standing with my giant

garbage bag of clothes and one accounting book. Since I'd soaked the floor, there was nowhere to put down my crap so I could run back upstairs for paper towels. So I opened the building's exterior door and kicked a rock in between it and the frame to prop it open, and ran to deposit my things in the trunk of my car.

When I got back inside, I kicked the rock out of the way and let the door slam shut as I tiptoed through it to fetch some paper towels. When I got what I needed, I ran back downstairs and bent to clean up the mess I'd made. I reached for the bubbly brown liquid that had spread past the mailboxes and was running under the door to the trash room.

That was when I felt a sharp pain explode in the back of my head, and everything went black.

CHAPTER 19

XANDER

I wasn't letting on that it hurt like hell to breathe. I was an actor, after all.

But I'd left the house a bit earlier than necessary to swing by an urgent care center for an X-ray or two. I'd not told Belle and certainly not the folks working on my movie. If necessary, I'd share the outcome with the stunt director to see if he could work around it, but until then, I was keeping it quiet.

Sure, Belle had seen me moving like an old man all day Saturday, despite the time I'd spent in the hot tub. But I'd convinced her it was soreness and nothing else.

Hopefully, I was right.

"Mr. Johnson?" a nurse called.

I followed her back to the room where they'd taken my X-ray.

"Looks like you're pretty sore, Mr. Johnson," she said, watching my slightly bent walk.

"It's that obvious?" I asked with a laugh. Which I instantly regretted. It hurt to laugh.

"Have a seat here," she said, pointing. "Okay, turns out you do not have any broken ribs—"

Yes.

"—but they were hit hard enough that you have some good bruises and spasming muscles. That's almost more painful than broken ribs would be."

"All right. That's good to hear, I guess. How long till I'm back to normal?"

"Probably a couple weeks or so."

Shit.

I returned to my car armed with muscle relaxers that, as a nice side effect, would knock a person on their ass. They'd kill the pain but could only be taken at bedtime, when I was prepared to sleep for a good eight to ten hours.

Unfortunately, I didn't have time for that and would have to get by on Advil and adrenaline. But at least I'd gotten good news—I wasn't broken. I started by drive toward the studio and dialed Belle.

My worry started when she didn't answer.

A burning stirred in my stomach. I'd asked her to keep her phone with her at all times. But she was probably just napping.

Right?

I set a reminder on my phone to try her again in an

hour and popped a couple of Advil. It wouldn't do for the studio to see me as the mess I was.

Thankfully it was an easy day of costume fittings, and I'd managed to spend most of my time sitting on my ass. I used being tired as an excuse for moving slowly, and no one knew any better.

But after the second phone reminder buzzed and still no answer from Belle, I knew something was up.

"Hey," I said to the wardrobe folks. "I have a family thing going on I need to take care of. Can we continue this tomorrow?"

"Sure, Xander," the lead costumer said. "Just make sure you're in early tomorrow to check your shoes for your fight scene."

When I got to my car, my heart was racing and I was just about in full-on panic mode. But I sucked in slow, deep breaths. It was not the time to lose my shit. I had to think clearly.

On my way back to Malibu, I dialed my buddy Sean. He would have good advice.

"Yo, Xander. How're you doing?"

"Sean. She's not answering her phone."

He took a deep breath. "Oh, Christ."

"I left her this morning, and I've been calling her all day."

"Holy shit. What can I do to help?" he asked.

"Not sure yet," I admitted. "I'm heading home right now."

"Okay. Call me when you get there," he said. "And

Xander, whatever you do, play it cool. If she forgot or broke her phone or some shit, play it cool. If it's not that...play it cool."

The Caddy wasn't really made for weaving in and out of traffic, but when I'd finally gotten to the freeway, I floored it, taking advantage of my eight-cylinder engine.

When I pulled up to the house, my fears were confirmed. The place was dark.

Completely fucking dark.

"Belle?" I shouted as soon as I was in the front door.

I ran as best I could with my sore ribs to the bedroom, where the cat meowed loudly, annoyed at having been woken from a nap. I looked out on the back deck.

Where was she?

I finally looked in the garage.

Her goddamn car was not there.

Shit, shit, shit. Where had she gone, and why wasn't she answering her phone?

I dialed the car dealership and asked for Jackie, hoping she was in.

"Xander? Is everything okay?" she asked.

"Jackie. I can't find Belle. Have you see her? Heard from her?"

"Oh my god." Her voice cracked. "I haven't spoken to her since I saw her Friday when you picked her up after work. I thought she was going to study all weekend."

"I left this morning to go to the studio. I haven't been able to get in touch with her all day."

"Have you tried her apartment?" she asked. "Maybe she forgot something?"

"That's where I'm going next."

"I'll meet you there," she said.

When I screeched into the lot where Belle's apartment was, Jackie pulled in right behind me.

Then I spotted the VW.

It was unlocked, so I got in it, searching for clues. I popped the trunk and ran around to the back.

"She must have come to pick up clothes. And look, there's one of her textbooks," Jackie said.

I looked around. Why would her car still be there? I spotted the lights on at the pizza place.

"C'mon."

Jackie followed me to the shop.

It was empty, save for the guy I guessed was the owner.

"Hi. Do you know Belle Thomas?"

He came out from the back, wiping his hands on his long white apron.

"Yeah. She's my neighbor. We live above this place," he said, pointing up. "She was here, I don't know—I guess a few hours ago."

Now we were making progress. Or so I hoped.

"Do you know where she went?" I asked.

He craned his neck around me and pointed to her

car in the lot. "Well, she must be in her apartment, if her car is here."

"I've been calling her all day and gotten no answer. She was supposed to stay at my house and not leave. She's in danger. We can't figure out why she'd come back here and why she isn't answering her phone."

The shop owner reached into his pocket, and his keys jingled. "C'mon. Let's go see if we can find anything. I'm Guy, by the way." He pulled the shop door closed behind him and locked the dead bolt.

The seconds we stood in front of the heavy metal door to Belle's building seemed like an eternity, while the shop owner fumbled with his keys. When he finally got the door open, he whistled softly.

"She bought that soda from me just before she went upstairs," Guy said, looking at the brown liquid that had run all the way across the small lobby floor. It had dried to a shiny, sticky mess and had obviously been undisturbed for some time. He bent to pick up the cup. "See, it has the pizzeria's name on it."

"Hey, check out the paper towels on the floor here," Jackie said, pointing.

"It looks like she might have been cleaning up the soda," I rasped, fear and anger filling my body.

"I'm calling the police," Jackie said, pulling out her cell.

"Let's look upstairs," Guy said.

The dingy hallway was quiet, and when we reached Belle's door, it was locked up tight.

I pounded on it anyway. "Belle! Are you in there?" I shouted.

"I've got an idea," Guy said. "I know the landlord. He'll let us in."

After fifteen minutes of frantic pacing and waiting for the LAPD to show up, Guy's landlord appeared with a key.

"You guys sure you want to do this? We're not supposed to just walk into apartments," he said nervously. "The cops show up, I gotta do some explaining."

I was in no mood for worrying about rules or regulations. "Open it. Now," I commanded.

Since I stood a good several inches taller than the landlord, he looked at me and then at Guy, who nodded for him to go ahead.

Belle's apartment looked fine from the doorway. I slowly entered with the others close behind.

"Belle?" I said quietly. "Are you here?"

I scanned the living room and kitchen and then moved to the bedroom.

"No sign of her. But her closet's open, and there are a pile of hangers here. She was definitely picking up more clothes."

Why hadn't she just waited for me to get home?

Two cops arrived in the apartment. "What's going on?" they asked.

"A friend of mine, Belle Thompson, is being stalked

by her ex-husband. And now she's missing," I said. "We're trying to find her."

"Are you sure?" one of them asked.

"Yes, I'm sure." I was trying to keep my voice steady as I filled them in on everything.

"Why hadn't she called the police before?" one of them asked.

Jackie spoke up. "She *has* called the police. Many times. In fact, last time she did, she ended up in the hospital, her face beaten to a pulp while your West Virginia brethren did jack shit to her ex." Her voice caught. "You aren't protecting her. You never have."

"Now ma'am, let's stay calm. We have to wait twenty-four hours before we open a missing persons report."

Now I understood why Belle didn't bother with cops. Even after hearing she'd been abused, they weren't doing a damn thing.

"Officers," I started, "it could not be more clear that she came by here to pick up some clothes and didn't make it out alone. There's no reason why her soda would be all over the lobby floor like that, or why she would not be answering her phone."

The police looked at me thoughtfully. "All right. Let's go down to the station."

The landlord locked up after us, and Jackie offered to follow the cops to the station.

I had other plans. I followed everyone to the station, too, but dialed Zenia on the way.

"Hello, darling," she said. "How is the movie business?"

"Zenia," I said, not mincing words, "I need your help with something."

All traces of amusement dropped from her voice, and she immediately went all business. "Xander, you sound terrible. What the hell is going on?"

"Zenia, Belle's missing." I nearly choked on the words.

"Oh god. Is it the ex?" she asked.

"I suspect it is. I need your help. I wouldn't ask you for this unless I were desperate. The cops...the cops can't do shit." We'd arrived at the police station, but I waved for Jackie to go ahead without me.

"Okay, honey. What do you need?"

"I know you have connections. I want someone to ping her cell phone," I said.

"Sweetie, you need a subpoena to do that. It's kind of a big deal."

"I know Zenia, I know. But you know lots of judges. And you know lots of cops. You've got to help me," I begged. "Whatever you need to do...I'll owe you."

"I'll do what I can. Let me make some calls."

I gave her Belle's phone number, then ran into the police station. I didn't have high hopes but figured it was best to work through the formal channels while pulling strings on the outside.

Jackie and I were in middle of giving the cops all

the info we had about Belle and her ex when my phone buzzed.

It was Zenia. I excused myself and hustled outside, as fast as my jacked-up ribs would let me.

"Xander. We found her. Wel, her phone anyway," she said.

Yes.

"Where is she?"

"Looks like she—well, her phone—is traveling east toward Las Vegas."

Cripes. I didn't know how I'd catch whoever she was with. But I could try.

I started the Caddy. Jackie could finish the police interview on her own.

"I'm hitting the road, Zenia."

"No need to do that, sweetie. Head over to the Hughes Heliport. I'll have a pilot waiting for you. It's the only way you'll catch them."

"Holy shit, Zenia. How will I ever repay you?" I sped through downtown traffic.

"You already have, sweetie. You are putting your life on the line for a lovely young woman. I've been in this town a long time...I think you're the first real action hero I've ever met. It's the least I can do."

I pulled into the heliport, jumped out of my car, and ran for their office.

"I'm Xander Johnson. Zenia Porter arranged a helicopter for me."

A young guy flipped papers on a clipboard.

"Gotcha right here. Let me take you to your ride, Mr. Johnson."

CHAPTER 20

BELLE

I came to, slowly, rolling back and forth, and back again. Gently at first, then violently, I only became fully awake when my head hit something hard and plastic. What the hell was happening?

The answer came quickly.

As did the terror. Sheer terror.

There was a strange pull, almost if gravity were out of whack, yanking random parts of my body in all directions.

Then, there was the smell. And the music. Familiar and yet strange. I knew where I was, and then I didn't.

I was submerged in total darkness, but as a certain fuzziness left me, I was able to identify where I was and why I was being tossed around like a rag doll.

And that smell. The goddamn smell. And the music

I'd hated for as long as I could remember—some country-rock hybrid thing that not only never made any sense, but also was the favorite of my ex-husband's.

Yeah, I knew where I was. And it was not a good place.

I tried to keep quiet, but something must have changed in the way I was moving. A moment later, he spoke.

"Oh, sleeping beauty is awake."

His voice made my hair stand on end. The fucker.

"Todd, why are you doing this?"

His reply was a nonsensical shriek, and I couldn't understand a single word of it.

But one thing I knew. I was blindfolded, and my hands and legs were tied. I was on the back seat floor of some car. And I was with my crazy, obsessive ex-husband.

Things were not looking good.

I managed to rub my head against something with enough catch to push my blindfold up an inch or two. I continued worming my head back and forth and managed to raise the blindfold to my eyebrows, far enough to be able to see.

Not that there was much to see. It was pitch-dark both in the car and out the windows, and when I craned my head to look outside, all I could see was the night and a few random, faraway stars.

We must have left the confines of L.A., because it would never be so dark there.

Where was the fucker taking me?

My life was over. All that running, and look—I ended up right back where I'd started, at the mercy of a man I hated. I wouldn't see my friends again, nor my job or apartment. No more college classes.

But what really got me was the thought of no more Xander. That's what took the lump in my throat and turned it into a breathy sob that I stifled against the floor of the car. Goddammit, it wasn't fair.

But I knew better than to expect life to be fair. It was anything but. Some people got breaks, and some people got the shit end of the stick. There was no rhyme or reason to it. And I had a feeling the rest of my life would be measured in hours. No more days, weeks, or months.

Todd would take care of that.

No, a little voice said inside me. He could only do that if I lay there like a victim. I would figure something out. Keep my shit together. Put up a fight. What was the worst that could happen? *If you're going to die either way, at least you died fighting.*

The fear in my heart was paralyzing, but then Xander entered my mind, almost as if he were right there whispering in my ear. I surged with hope.

Todd continued to rant incoherently. Maybe I could snap him out of it?

"Todd, are you okay?" I took a deep breath, forcing myself to sound as supportive and sweeter than milk chocolate. "Todd, sweetie, tell me what's going on."

"Shut up. Shut up, you slut," he hissed. He started ranting again, and this time I was at least able to string together some of what he was saying.

He'd lost his mind, obviously. If I could keep it together and think straight, I might be able to make something happen. Xander, in the short time I'd known him, had shown me a man could be strong without being a violent asshole—that a real man could listen to and respect a woman without feeling diminished himself.

Unlike Todd.

There was so much I'd not known about him until a couple of years into our marriage. In public, he was the perfect partner. Tall, serious, and straight-laced, he could make you smile with an unexpected burst of humor. He was massively successful at work, loved and respected by all his colleagues.

Little did they know what he was like at home. And when I finally left him, and all his connections could no longer protect him, word spread through town like wildfire,. He lost his job and everything. I didn't feel badly for him, but in his sick, twisted mind, it was my fault, so he hunted me down. I was the one who would have to pay.

And all I'd wanted was to get the hell out of Dodge.

"How did you find me, Todd?" I tried working the bindings on my wrists, but they were tight. So very tight.

The ranting had faded. "I know people. Of course I

was going to find you. Did you really think you could get away? Leave me and my life in a shambles? No, Belle, we were married. That's a commitment. For life."

I was desperate. Ready to try anything.

"I...I'm sorry, Todd. Could we try again? Would you give me another chance?"

Silence filled the air for what seemed like a long time.

"I don't know. Do you mean that?" he asked.

"Of course," I lied between clenched teeth as I madly searched for anything rough enough to start wearing through the tape around my wrists. "I've missed you. I was just afraid you'd be so mad, I stayed away. I didn't realize...how much you still loved me. And...how much I loved you."

I held my breath. It was probably the worst acting job of all time, but I was willing to say whatever I had to. I was going to fight and be strong. And if I got out alive, I was going to make some big changes in my life, starting with really buckling down and finishing school. All I needed was one shot, one chance.

The clarity that an up-close experience with terror brought was life-altering.

"Yeah."

"What, Todd? I'm sorry, baby, but this is a little tight back here. What did you say?"

"Yes, I'll take you back. But we have to go someplace new, where no one knows of my past. I had to leave town all because of you and your big mouth."

I wanted to argue and scream at him and point out that his buddies had covered for him until they couldn't any longer. I'd just left town quietly and disappeared. Or, tried to.

No, I was going to keep all that to myself for the time being.

"I'm pulling over to get gas. Keep your mouth shut, or you'll be sorry. There are a lot of desert animals in these parts that would love to make a meal of you."

I shivered at the cold in his voice as he slammed the car door, and squirmed around to find a sharp edge to work my bindings...

CHAPTER 21

XANDER

I'd never been in a helicopter and would have preferred my first time been something other than hunting down my girl and her crazy ex.

That's right, *my* girl. I was done playing around with it in my mind. Belle was mine. She'd given herself to me, and I would move heaven and earth to keep her safe.

As the helicopter flew east and the lights of L.A. faded behind us, there was nothing ahead but dark desert.

"How will we find them?" I asked.

"Don't worry. There aren't a lot of cars out at this hour, and there's only I-15 to Vegas. We'll call Zenia to check in with her contact in a few minutes. We'll have to do some guessing, but we'll get close," the pilot said.

I looked over at him. "Close isn't good enough."

He shook his head. "I know. I've got the throttles on this thing full out, and we're pushing a hundred and fifty right now. I used to do shit like this all the time in the military. We'll catch up."

Fuck. If something happened to Belle—something more than had already happened, that was—I could never forgive myself. I'd promised her she'd be safe, and I'd let her down.

And as painful as my ribs were, I couldn't wait to get my hands on her asshole ex. That fucker was going to be sorry he'd gotten out of bed in the morning.

"Hey, I'm getting a call." Something was coming in over the pilot's headset, and he replied into the small mic next to his mouth.

He turned to me. "It looks like they just pulled into a gas station right up there. See the lights?" he asked, pointing toward the lone block of light in an otherwise black night. Off in the distance behind it I could see a few other lights, but it was obvious, this was a small-town station that probably doubled as a truck stop. "Awesome. This fucker never stood a chance."

"Where are you going to put the helicopter down?" I asked.

"See the road in front? I'm gonna drop her right at the entrance to the gas station. Can't let him get away, can we?" The pilot grinned, clearly enjoying his mission.

I held my breath as we got closer. There were a few

cars below us, and I couldn't be sure which one Belle was in.

I had the side door of the helicopter open even before he touched down, jumping out and running toward the gas pumps. All eyes had turned to see the helicopter land in front of the gas station. And most people looked confused. Except for one guy, who was quickly putting his gas cap back on.

"Excuse me, sir," I called.

He glanced in my direction for a second and then acted like he'd never heard me. Just as he started to climb into his car and pull the door closed, I wedged myself in the opening, grabbed him by the collar, and yanked him out of the car. Just as I did, I spotted a terrified Belle in the back on the floor.

As much as my side hurt, I grabbed the guy around the waist and lifted him up and slammed him to the concrete with every ounce of my body, probably causing him more pain than anything he'd ever felt. He screamed as blood poured from his nose down the front of his clothes, pooling on the asphalt below. Not satisfied he was truly incapacitated, I gripped the hair on the back of his head and smashed his face against the ground. If his nose wasn't busted before, it certainly was then.

With him down, I turned to the car and pulled the door open to get Belle. I lifted her to sit on the back seat, and with the help of a knife sitting on the front passenger seat, cut her restraints.

As soon as her hands were freed, she threw her arms around me and the sobs started.

"I knew you'd come," she said, in between heaves. "I knew you'd help me, one way or the other."

I held her tight. I had my Belle back again. "You're safe now, baby. I'm here."

Sirens wailed in the distance, and I knew Zenia had gotten the highway patrol involved. I looked to where the ex was on the ground, still bleeding. He kept trying to stand but would tumble back to his hands and knees. He'd go to prison this time, for sure.

"How'd you find me?" she asked as I carried her away from the vehicle. Someone started to ask what was going on but stopped when they saw the scraps of tape still hanging from her wrists.

"Believe it or not, it was pretty much all Zenia's doing."

"What do you mean?" she asked.

"She was able to get someone to track your cell, and they figured out you were heading in the direction of Vegas. She lined up a helicopter so we could come get you."

Her red eyes widened. "She did that for you?"

I shook my head. "She did it for us."

"Are you okay to walk?" I asked. I would hold her forever if she wanted, but my ribs were starting to wake up, and I could use a bit of a break.

"Yeah, I think so. I'm pretty sure he whacked me here." She winced when she touched what looked like a growing bump on the back of her head and leaned on me as I walked her over to sit on a curb.

"Why'd you leave the house, Belle? I thought you promised to stay in?"

She looked down at her hands and shook her head. "It was stupid. So stupid of me. The outcome could have been so much worse."

I took a deep breath. Whatever had caused her to leave—clothes, a book, whatever—it wasn't important.

"It doesn't matter. You're safe now."

"I'm sorry, Xander. You've done so much for me, and I screwed this up."

She shivered from the chilly desert night. I kissed her on the forehead and pulled her close. On the other side of the parking lot, the cops were handcuffing Todd.

"Look at him," she said. "To think I once loved that man. And now he's going to jail."

"Yup. He brought you over a state line. That's a federal offense. He's in deep shit," I said.

"Ma'am, are you okay to talk for a bit?" a female officer asked after Todd was taken away. "We need a statement from you for an arrest."

Belle let go of me and stood up, squaring her shoulders. "Of course."

The cop nodded and pulled out a notepad, trying to remain casual but professional.

"Can you tell us everything that happened?" she

asked. "It's okay to ramble, we'll be able to sort it out later."

In slow, almost controlled bursts of words, Belle recounted how she'd gone to her old apartment, and on the way out, Todd had knocked her out and thrown her in the back of his rental car.

To see my girl out of danger was the best feeling I'd ever had. For a moment, all was right with the world—well, at least as right as it could get.

CHAPTER 22

BELLE

Xander returned from inside the gas station with a tray of coffees. With so many different departments involved, it seemed that paperwork on this would take forever. There had even been a comment about the FAA getting involved. But Xander was patient, and his patience helped me keep it together.

He handed me a coffee, and then one to each of the police officers. I shifted the bag of ice he'd gotten for the back of my head.

The male officer spoke up.

"Ma'am, we found bomb materials in the car. We're not sure what his plan was, but you're very lucky your friend here moved fast."

I knew I was lucky, very freaking lucky. I squeezed Xander's hand.

"There was also a letter," the officer said.

"A letter? What do you mean?" I asked.

"Looks like he intended to drive cross-country to your former home in West Virginia. He was going to burn the house down with the two of you in it."

"Jesus Christ," Xander growled. "What a sick fuck."

That about summed it up. And even thought I was finally safe, I couldn't stop shaking.

"You've been through quite a lot, Ms. Thomas. I suggest you take it easy for a while. It doesn't seem like you need a hospital or anything, so we'll leave you in the hands of your friend here, if that is okay."

"Hey," Xander said, when the cops had left.

"Yeah?"

"It's time to go home."

I nodded toward the helicopter. "Is that how we're getting home?"

"Would you rather walk?" he asked with a laugh.

"Well, now I think you're just showing off," I said with a sly smile.

"*What?*"

"You know, we haven't even been going out that long, and already you're taking me for a helicopter ride."

He helped me step up into the helicopter as the pilot held the door for us.

"I think you're the one taking *me* for a ride. We wouldn't be here if it weren't for you."

"All right, Mr. Hollywood," I laughed.

"Hey, I like the sound of that."

We buckled in, and the helicopter took off, leaving behind the desert, vast and dark in the night. The lights of L.A. twinkled as we got closer, and by the time we were just a few miles out, the horizon exploded with light like the billboards in Times Square. After the black of the desert, I had to blink as my eyes adjusted.

"Beautiful, isn't it?" Xander asked.

"It's amazing. Look at the cars snaking up the freeway. It looks so peaceful from here."

He laughed. "Well, we'll be in the thick of it in just a short while. Prepare yourself."

"As long as I'm with you, the L.A. traffic won't bother me a bit."

He leaned over and planted a kiss on my temple, but not without wincing.

"Oh my god, you're still in pain."

He nodded. "Don't sweat it, I got X-rays. My ribs are fine. Just a few muscle spasms."

"Okay. Soon as we get you home, I'm going to help take your mind off your injuries. As soon as I take aspirin for my little headache." Naturally, I emphasized my promise with a sly little smile.

Our helicopter landed with a thud, and after shutting down, the pilot opened the door to let us exit.

"Thanks, dude," Xander said, giving him the half-shake half-hug guy thing.

"Take care, you guys," he called after us. "Stay out of trouble."

I planned to. Oh, I planned to.

After probably the craziest freaking day of my life, I was back at Xander's place.

First, I checked in with Jackie to let her know I was home safe and sound. Then, I called Nina, who was so happy she sobbed at the other end of the line.

I pulled Xander outside to the hot tub for a little soak.

"Take a seat," I told him and watched him slowly lean back onto lounge chair opposite me.

I'd showered to get the day's trauma off, so was wearing only the oversized robe I'd pretty much stolen from him. I stood before him, really only inches from where he sat, and lowered it down my shoulders. A smile grew across his face, and if I wasn't mistaken, so did the cock in his jeans.

"Is baby gonna get naked for me?" he mused.

"You want me to?" I teased.

His gaze ran over me. It was clear he wanted the goods, regardless of his ribs. "Drop the robe," he demanded.

Who was I to say no? I let it slither to the deck in a puddle.

"Now you," I said.

"Me?"

"C'mon. Stand up. I'll help you out of your clothes."

Wincing, his pushed himself to his feet. I lifted the faded rock concert T-shirt over his head, taking care to stay away from his sore side.

God, he was freaking hot, standing there barefoot and shirtless, wearing only some tattered old blue jeans that hung low around his hips. His ribs were rightly black and blue, but it just made him hotter as I sank to my knees.

I reached for the fly of his jeans and eased the zipper down, our gazes locked. His lips were pressed together, and his blue eyes drilled into mine as I grasped the hard cock that sprang from his pants. With my other hand, I pushed his jeans over his ass and down to the floor, where he stepped out of them.

Since I was already on my knees, I took advantage of the opportunity to taste him. I pulled him toward my mouth, and while I licked the shiny drop of precum off him, kept my gaze on his.

"Mmmm. Tastes good, baby," I said.

"Yeah? You liking my cock, darlin'?"

I didn't think that question needed answering. I just smiled and took him as far in my mouth as I could, tightening my lips for suction and pulling them along his length until all I held was his head. Just like I'd seen in the pornos.

Hey, those movies served their purpose.

"God, baby can suck cock," he said.

Well, I didn't need much more encouragement than that, so I took him as deeply as I could again, cradling his balls in one hand, the other holding him by the root.

The beach breeze slithered over me, such a welcome treat after a horrendous past twenty-four hours. Xander's eyes closed as the moon illuminated his beautiful face.

"Fuck, baby, you're gonna make me come."

I drew him deeper and pistoned his length, each time sucking the head of his cock until my cheeks hollowed and his legs quivered. His hands held my head, and as he got closer, he fucked my mouth until my eyes teared and I was close to choking.

"Oh fuck!" he bellowed, pumping his hips into my mouth as I took every drop of the cum he shot down my throat.

He pulled me up and planted light kisses on the sides of my face. "C'mon. Let's get in the hot tub."

We held hands as we lowered ourselves into the hot, steamy bubbles. He closed his eyes as the water lapped around his midsection, and he slowly sank onto the hot tub's bench seat and relaxed.

"You feeling okay?" I asked.

He dropped his head back onto the edge of the tub

and took a deep breath. "Fucking awesome, actually. I got the blowie of a lifetime out on my deck, and now I'm in a hot tub that's relaxing me more by the minute. I was just wondering if I've really hit my head and this is all a fantasy."

He looked over and smiled at me. "What a kickass woman you are."

If my heart could have left my body, it would have soared somewhere far above where life was always perfect and beautiful. Holy shit.

"But...I think I want something," he said. "And to give you something, baby."

"What?" I asked, intrigued.

"Come over here," he murmured, his eyes fiery with desire.

I waded across to him.

He patted the underwater bench where he was sitting. "Rest your foot here." He pulled my foot until it rested right next to his hip and then pulled me closer by placing his hands on my ass until my pussy was nearly in his face. Which I guess was the point. He reached out and kissed my tummy, and I held his shoulders for balance.

When his tongue flicked the top of my slit, I gripped him more tightly. And when he reached my clit, which by now extended beyond my pussy lips, I dropped my head back as sensation exploded in every pore. I couldn't help myself and pushed deeper into his mouth.

He spread me with his fingers and drove his tongue

deeper into my cleft. My legs wobbled, and I dropped my head back as an orgasm crashed into me like a speeding train.

"God, Xander. I'm coming, baby." I couldn't speak any louder than a whisper as my body convulsed.

When my orgasm wound down, I was as limp as a rag doll. I put one knee on either side of Xander's hips and snuggled into his wet arms, kissing his head and neck.

"Hey," he said.

"Yeah?"

"You want to come to the studio with me tomorrow? Watch for a little while?"

"Can I? I have the day off. Jackie took care of that for me. Won't I be in the way?"

Would I see movie stars? Actually, I had a soon-to-be movie star right in front of me. Who I was naked with. In his hot tub.

"There's a spot where guests hang out so they don't get in the way. You'll be fine. Oh...and it's right by the catering table. I heard they specialize in oatmeal cookies."

"Really? Oh my god, that sounds so cool. I'd love to!"

My mind wandered to the next important decision I had to make.

What would I wear?

CHAPTER 23

XANDER

It was so early the sun wasn't even up yet, but the movie business was pretty much 24/7. If they wanted me there at six a.m., I'd be there at six a.m. Unfortunately, that meant Belle had to get up that early, too.

She yawned loudly. "Will they have coffee?"

I laughed. "Of course. And more."

"Oh, the sky is so pretty. I hate to think of all the sunrises I've missed in my life," she said.

"Well, you've got to sleep sometime. Hey, I was thinking."

"Yeah? Of what?"

"I'd like to help you go to school full-time. You know, you could finish your studies without having work get in the way."

She reached across the bed and squeezed my hand. "Oh my god, that is so sweet. I could never accept such an offer, but, thank you."

I had a feeling her first answer would be *no*.

"Geez. You could at least consider it," I said, stealing a glance at her.

Despite my best intentions, I kept picturing how hot she looked with my cock down her throat the night before.

Down, boy. Not before costume fitting and rehearsals.

"I didn't mean to sound ungrateful. It's just that I need to make my own way. It's part of getting out of that horrendous relationship I was in for so long."

"Okay. I get it. But if you change your mind and want to be a full-time student, let me know."

She laughed. "And how the hell would I pay my rent? That job at the car dealership is not a great one, but it pays my bills."

"Well, maybe you won't have to pay rent anymore."

"Huh?"

"Move in with me permanently. Ditch the apartment."

She turned to me in total surprise, a grin spreading on her beautiful face. "Um, what? And leave behind my glamorous existence living above a pizza joint in a strip mall?"

I nodded. "I know how happy that place makes you. Geez, what was I thinking?"

I bit my tongue to keep from laughing.

"Well, now that you know what a high-rent girl I am, you won't make such silly suggestions going forward," she said with a giggle.

"Hey, lesson learned. I ain't no dummy. But maybe you'll come visit me here in Malibu every once in awhile?"

"Hmmm." She looked out the window. "I don't know. I mean, a huge, modern house on the beach with killer views. I just don't know if I'm down with that."

"All right. After today I'll just drop you off on my way home. We can go our separate ways. Okay?"

"Ha. You think you can get rid of me that easily?" she asked.

When the horny director saw me with Belle, she backed off about a thousand percent. I was impressed, actually. Some vipers like her got their kicks out of cockblocking other women.

She had integrity, it seemed. Too much libido, but integrity. I respected that.

With Belle safely ensconced in the visitor area, I ran over my lines with the starlet—the one who was supposed to be the next Gwyneth Paltrow. Only thing was, poor girl, she was such a nervous wreck she'd almost been fired twice.

The movie industry was unforgiving that way.

We'd run our lines together several times, and I

thought we were pretty much ready. All cameras were trained on us as the director called, *roll*.

I moved in on her, a love interest named Bettina. I ran my hands through her hair and said my first line.

"I love you, Belle. I really do."

"*Cut*," the director screamed.

"What? What happened?" I asked.

She sighed loudly and put her hands on her hips. "You said *Belle*, not *Bettina*. Come on, let's roll it again."

Oh shit. Had I done that? I looked over to Belle, whose face was beet red.

Well, that was one way to let a girl know how you felt.

When we broke for lunch, I walked with her to the canteen.

"Hey, what you said back there. When you flubbed your line. Do you get in trouble for that sort of thing?" she asked.

I tilted my head. "Depends. Depends on how bad a mistake it was. Or whether it was a mistake at all."

"What do you mean?"

"Well. I didn't intend to blurt out *I love you, Belle*, but it couldn't have been a complete accident."

She swallowed hard. "Um…what?"

I shrugged. "It was just as good a time as any to tell you how I felt."

Her eyes widened. "You really feel that way?"

"I do. I love you, Belle."

Her eyes filled with tears. "If I say it, will you think it's a mistake?"

"Depends on how you say it. And who you say it to," I said.

"Okay. Because I love you, too."

CHAPTER 24

XANDER

It took us a few days to get over to The Agency, but when we did, Zenia got up from her desk and rushed to greet us. "Belle, I haven't seen you since... well, your first visit here." She gave her a warm hug.

"Good to see you, too, Zenia. I don't know how I can ever repay you for all you did for me. You saved my life. Truly."

Zenia waved her hand in a *no big deal* gesture.

"I'm so glad my connections paid off." Zenia looked over at me and smiled. "Thank god you're both safe. If I never have another chance to help in such a situation, I'll consider this the most important thing I've done in my life."

Belle's hand flew to her mouth. I had to admit, I teared up a bit, too.

"Thank you, Zenia. From the bottom of our hearts," I said.

She leaned back in her chair. "You know, you guys are really cute together. Both good-looking blondies. You'll make cute babies."

"What?" Belle said, looking confused.

I patted her arm. "Oh, Zenia's always cutting up. Aren't you, Zenia?" I gave her my best, discreet stink eye. I'd get even with her later. She grinned, while I reached into my coat pocket for the envelope we needed to bring by.

"So Zenia, back to business. This is my formal resignation from The Agency. It's been a whirlwind of good times and hard lessons. I wouldn't do a thing any differently, if I had it to do all over."

She nodded. "I'm glad to hear that, sweetie. And I wouldn't do a thing differently either. I've not met as many people with your integrity, Xander."

She turned to Belle. "You got a good one, my friend."

Belle nodded. "I know. 'Course, he isn't doing too badly, himself."

Zenia laughed, and I gave Belle an amused look.

"So, I have a proposition for you, Xander. I'd like to be your agent," Zenia said. "After all, you did say you owed me one, and quite frankly, honey, that stiff you've got now couldn't do half of what I can for you."

"Really?" I ask, shocked. "What about The Agency? And why wouldn't you aim for a real star? You know, someone whose career is established? You certainly have the experience and connections to do that."

"First, The Agency is on autopilot thanks to Sean's work. It's incredibly successful, and I find I have a bit more time on my hands these days. Second, you're going places, my friend. There's no reason to work with someone whose career is established when you can be part of a rising star."

"Zenia. I don't know what to say, except thank you. That's a compliment of the highest order. Wow." I was pretty much speechless. And flattered, of course.

"Just tell me you'll think about it."

"I will. Absolutely." I stopped, then shook my head and offered her my hand. "No need to think on it."

On our way out of Zenia's office, we ran smack into Sean.

I pulled him into a bear hug. "Dude. How can I ever thank you. I mean, you helped save my girl."

"It's all good, man. And this must be the lovely Belle. Good to meet you," he said, smiling.

"Yes, Sean. Good to meet you, too, and thank you." She pulled him into a hug of her own.

"Where you guys off to?" he asked.

I stole a peek at Belle. "Someplace special. Where it all began."

"Enjoy," he said, sending us on our way.

When we arrived at House of Waffles, Belle squealed with joy. "Oh my god. I've missed this place!"

We settled into her favorite booth.

"What did you think of Zenia's offer?" I asked, after we'd ordered burgers and fries.

"It's amazing. Just great." She stuffed several curly fries into her mouth.

"Yeah. It is amazing. And I have an offer, too. Of my own."

She took a sip of her soda. "Yeah? What's that?"

"I thought you might like to marry me."

She stopped chewing, her mouth full of fries.

"Huhhh?" was all she could say.

"Though you might like to, you know, tie the knot with me. Get hitched. Get married. I wanted to ask you here, in this special place."

It wasn't every day you asked someone to marry you, and it wasn't every day you did it at House of Waffles. But the moment Belle started nodding so hard her hair flew around her face, I realized I'd done the right thing.

I jumped over to her side of the booth so I could kiss her, which I did with a passion I'd never known I could muster. Two waitresses on the other side of the room smiled and nudged each other.

"I love you, you know," she said, as we parted for air.

"Hey, don't I get points for being the first to say it?" I teased.

"Not really. First it was an accident. And second, I don't care who gets points. I just want you."

Thank you for reading Belle's story.
If you enjoyed it, please leave a review on:

Amazon

Billionaires

The Billionaire's Secret

eBook

Paperback

The Billionaire's Betrayal

eBook

Paperback

CONTACT MIKA LANE

Stay in the know
NEVER pay full price for a new release.
Join my Insider Group
Be the first to hear about private $.99 release specials,
giveaways, other great authors to read, the opportunity
to receive advance reader copies (ARCs), and other
random musings.

Let's keep in touch
Contact me here
Visit me! www.mikalane.com
Friend me! Facebook
Pin me! Pinterest
Follow me! Twitter

ABOUT THE AUTHOR

About me

Writing has been a passion of mine since, well, forever (my first book was "The Day I Ate the Milkyway," a true fourth-grade masterpiece), but steamy romance is now what gives purpose to my days and nights. I live in magical Northern California with my own handsome alpha dude, sometimes known as Mr. Mika Lane, and an evil cat named Bill. A lover of shiny things, I've been known to try to new recipes on unsuspecting friends, find hiding places so I can read undisturbed, and spend my last dollar on a plane ticket somewhere. I also drink cheap champagne and have way too many shoes.

A National Reader's Choice Awards finalist, I'll always promise you a hot, sexy romp with kick-ass but imperfect heroines, and some version of a modern-day happily ever after.

I LOVE to hear from readers when I'm not dreaming up naughty tales to share. Join my Insider Group so we can get to know each other better. Or contact me here.

18764392R00146

Made in the USA
San Bernardino, CA
21 December 2018